MEMORY TOUCHES MEMORY

Though born in Birmingham, Alabama, John Lee Weldon has been for the best of his life a native of New York City. He is the author of numerous best selling novels, most notably *The Naked Heart* (Farrar, Strauss and Young) and *Thunder in the Heart* (New American Library).

The last thirty years have established him as a leading light on New York's literary scene. Set in the fifties, *Memory Touches Memory* represents a return to his theme of romantic intensity. It his first work to be published in the UK.

MEMORY TOUCHES MEMORY

JOHN LEE WELDON

GMP

First published August 1989 by
GMP Publishers Ltd,
PO Box 247, London N17 9QR

World Copyright © John Lee Weldon 1989

Distributed in North America by
Alyson Publications Inc.,
40 Plympton St, Boston, MA 02118, USA

British Library Cataloguing in Publication Data
Weldon, John Lee,
Memory Touches Memory.
I. Title
813'.54 [F]

ISBN 0-85449-114-7

Printed and bound in the European Community by
Norhaven A/S, Viborg, Denmark

FOR THE MEMORY OF LEN W.

The first and highest law must be
the love of man to man.

— Ludwig Feuerbach
German philosopher

— 1804-1872

Chapter 1

A YOUNG MAN will be here soon. He can't be more than twenty. Do I dare to dream the dream of gay dreamers?

I gaze into the heart of memory – everyone's heart is overflowing with memories – and in my heart I see myself as a young man.

This is another self I see – a self of another time, another age, the self of my youth.

There is a mirror in everyone's heart.

I peer deep into this mirror and I realize we are made of many mirrors – the mirror of the soul and the mirror of the flesh, and I see the reflection of many men – the men of my youth.

They have never left me – Memory and Dreams have that much in common.

Oh, yes, in the reality of time they left me or I left them, chances are we left each other, but something of their blood, their love, their near-love, almost love, some touch, some element of themselves, came into me, and lined my internal self with a coating of reflective dreams.

Especially one man.

My heart takes comfort in memory.

No, I am not living entirely in the past, but there is something about youth that yearns, longs and needs love more fervently than a man of my mature years. I can, for the most part, especially in this day and age, content myself with the love of my dog and my books, my VCR, my creative spirit, the museums, and, yes, I cherish my memories.

I thank God I am gay.

I thank God for the many experiences I have had, not only

the love affairs, but the memories in my heart and soul reflect those brief episodes of supreme intimacies with intimate strangers whose names I never knew, for when I knew them, I needed only their lips and their flesh.

In truth, perhaps I have always needed, or thought I needed, more than the world and the moon and the stars could possibly give, but there are times when the need for fleeting intimacies serve me very well. Years pass, and perhaps I pass them on the street, and we do not even recognize each other, for memory has given them eternal youth in my eyes. Youth, of course, is a thing we place too much emphasis upon. And the public is guilty of trying to make the elderly older than they are. I have my own guilt, but it is a lilting-guilt; so I trust the gods shall not punish me for it. (How good it is to forgive one's own self for one's shortcomings.) Time has punished anyone I have ever known, over and over again. There are times when Time is the Devil. And I have had to struggle to forgive myself for more than one death, the death of someone I knew, and even the death of someone I did not know, someone I never met.

No matter what, all in all, memory serves me well. Oh, of course it is not the same as arms reaching towards each other and searching for touches of entrenched ecstasises, erectile dreams so intense for consummation that the moisture of youth lubricates the flesh while the mind drifts into a daze of non-thinking, only feeling the feelings of each other.

I cannot count the times when my mind seemed to melt into the fluids of my flesh. Times of caring only for the flesh, and that certainly was not always wise, but the wisdom of my mature years does not condemn the wild and eager passions of my youth.

Memory commends.

And memory commences:

8

Chapter 2

MY MOST BEAUTIFUL lover was Terry, Terry Lane. We met at a literary cocktail party, one of those parties I used to become excited about, but now shun. I no longer drink and I no longer care for crowds. But then:

There was that beuatiful man, about twenty-seven I guessed, holding a cocktail in one hand and a cigarette in the other, smiling as though the smile were real and not just a party smile. His teeth were white and even; his lips were moist and red. I felt a slight quivering of my flesh, and I was aware of a coating of perspiration between my buttocks. He was a blond, a light shade of unobtrusive yellow, and his complexion was light but definitely not pale. I could sense the blood of his flesh. I tightened my buttocks and let my fantasies run wild.

And then I saw the wedding ring on his third finger left hand, and I cursed under my breath in my cocktail, but I knew I would not let that foolish ring stand in my way. If his wife was there at the party, I did not see her, I did not meet her, and I did not want to meet her. My intentions were for only a momentary fling; my thoughts were only for a moment.

I had just lived through one love affair that had lasted only two months, and I liked to have a good six months of intense promiscuity between love affairs.

We do not always do as we intend to do. Our intentions are sometimes overpowered.

I was aware of the overpowering beauty of Terry Lane before I met him. I was aware of my heart giving me trouble with my throat and my stomach, to say nothing of what my fantasies were doing to my crotch, but I was wearing briefs so it did not show, at least not very much, but it was becoming as uncomfortable as hell, burning hell, I might add.

My God, how I wanted that beautiful man!

I never considered myself as being beautiful, but I was aware that there was a certain attractiveness about me, else how could I have known so many intimate encounters.

I was twenty-three at the time. I am five feet nine, and I guessed at Terry being about five eight. I was slender, almost too thin, and my cheeks were gaunt. Terry was of medium build. I have black hair with a slight wave. My lips have known many lips, so that says something about my lips. I am proud of my eight inches of projection, and through the cocktails I was letting my imagination measure Terry. (But in those days imagination was not enough for me – I was gathering future-memories, not recalling memories.) I let my glance examine his crotch. He was not wearing briefs, he was wearing shorts. I was pleased with what I saw.

He was talking with Walter and Vera when I stole that intimate glance at him, but I had a feeling he was aware of my eyes. Something started to grow. He put out his cigarette, stuck his hand in his left pocket and held it down.

Walter and Vera Smothers were close friends of mine. Walter's mind and heart were gay, but he was afraid to let his body be gay. He sublimated his feelings by working in the arts and gathering a number of gay friends around him. This must have tortured his soul. He drank too much and clenched his jaws too frequently. I wondered if Vera knew. I wondered if she ever realized that when he held her in his arms he was wanting to hold one of his gay friends. When Walter talked excitedly, as he was now doing with Terry, bubbles gathered at the corners of his lips. Walter's heart rode his mind in the direction of what he wanted, but his fears skidded on a slippery soul and skirted away, yet never all the way away.

Vera was lovely. She was in her late twenties. Her hair was dirty blond. She was from South Carolina and retained a slight Southern accent. She was quietly spoken. She was a lady in every sense of the word. If she knew anything about the insides of her husband, she was great at pretending not to know.

Walter Smothers was slightly over six feet tall. He was not yet fat, but he was heading in that direction. He was an attractive man, and if I had not felt closer to Vera than I felt toward him, I might have made a play for him. He, too, could not let go of his Southern accent. He was from Georgia, and he was in his early thirties.

I had mulled around at that party long enough. I knew what I wanted. I knew I had to have it and believed I could get it. I decided to barge in on the conversation Walter and Vera were having with the man I wanted.

"Phillip," Vera's voice lilted my way when I stepped over to them.

"Hello, Phillip," Walter said. "I was just telling Terry – have you met? Terry Lane, this is Phillip Tucman – I was telling Terry he should read Proust."

"Walter believes everyone should read Proust," Vera said. "But he forgets that everyone doesn't love literature as much as he does, and can't or won't take that much time to read big long Proust."

Walter generally talked more about a handful of gay writers than he did about a world full of straight writers.

"I'm not much at reading," Terry said, not yet looking at me directly in the eyes. "I am much more into living than I am at reading."

Now he looked into my eyes, only briefly, but I saw what I wanted to see. I saw desire. And I saw the most beautiful green eyes, the clearest green eyes, I have ever seen. They were jewels. They were more beautiful than emeralds. They were alive. It was then, at that moment, in those few seconds, that my heart told me this might be more than the flesh – whether or not I wanted more than the flesh – for the heart sometimes can be just as demanding as the genitals.

We were not even touching. As we were introduced, we did not shake hands. We simply nodded. He did not set his cocktail down or shift it to his other hand – he kept that hand in his left pocket. Yet, not touching, not even having touched, I felt I could feel his blood flowing through his veins.

"But literature lasts longer than anyone's life?" Walter Smothers often insisted upon the superiority of art over 'that stuff called humanity'.

I tried not to believe Walter.

But when the nights were blue, when the bed was empty, I would remember those words of Walter's and try to put them out of my memory.

Then at the party I let Walter's remark pass without comment, and I listened to Terry: "Longevity is not that important. What we are doing with time is more important than time itself."

I could see Vera's expression that she wanted to agree openly with Terry, but she was one of those wives who rarely disagree with her husband. She was raised that way.

"But time," Walter insisted, "is lost without the arts to record it."

"And we are lost if we don't live it," Terry smiled. His hand was still in his pocket, and I thought I saw it tighten.

"What is living?" Vera asked. (I believe she lived her whole life asking that question.)

"Doing what you want to do. And enjoying it," Terry replied, and there was joy in his tone of voice.

"Most people can't do what they want to do," Walter said. "Most people are stuck. Just stuck. And as far as enjoying what they do, the world is full of guilt, full of too much guilt to let people be free enough to do what they want to do."

"Now Walter," Vera laughed, falsely and nervously, "you don't want your freedom from me, do you?"

"Of course not. Don't be silly." There was something cruel about the way he said it. "I'm talking about internal freedom. Freedom from the Gods, or freedom from just one God, if there is one, or freedom from the years of guilt that society piles upon itself, generation after generation."

"I insist upon being my own society," Terry said, and strangely enough, there was a certain humility in his insistence. (His wedding ring was not visible. His hand was still in his pocket.)

"What in heaven's name do you mean by that?" Vera asked.

"My thoughts about myself and how I live my life are more

important to me than society's interpretations. That does not mean I am better than society in general. It simply means I am aware of my right to individual freedom, even if the world wants to make itself one huge prison. I am free within that prison, but that prison is not my prison. Freedom is not primarily an internal feeling. I am free because my thoughts are free."

"What does your wife think about that?" Walter asked.

"My wife accepted my feelings before she agreed to marry me. I told her everything I knew about myself. I told her that God and I created myself and that she could not re-create me. She agreed not to even try. We have been married six years now, and she hasn't yet begun to try. I don't believe she will."

(Was he telling me he was free to be with me?)

"Do you have any children?" Vera asked.

"We have two sons. Terry, Jr. is five. Ronald is four. If I want to go out for some reason, for instance, this party – I need a party now and then – she stays with the children. If she wants to go out shopping or with one of her girlfriends, I stay home with the boys. We love each other enough to respect each other's independence."

"Sometimes independence almost frightens me," Vera spoke in hardly more than a whisper.

"What?" Walter asked, not quite snapping.

"Oh, I didn't mean that. Did I?" and there was her slightly nervous laugh again.

(I was glad I was not married to Walter.)

"You need security," Terry continued, "to have real independence. Independence without security can be no more than a dressed-up bag lady or a street urchin in a top hat." I realized I had been too quiet because I was more and more fascinated by Terry Lane. He not only had a beautiful body, but he had something in that handsome head on his shoulders. I broke my silence: "You sound more emotionally mature than anyone I have ever met."

"Emotional maturity is finding yourself and respecting what you find."

"Suppose," Walter asked, "you like what you find but what you find frightens you?" That was Walter from top to bottom.

"Then you are losing yourself," Terry replied.

And then sadly from Walter: "I suppose most of the people of the world spend most of their lives losing themselves and trying to find themselves."

"Isn't life an eternal search?" I asked.

"It is," Terry said, "but it does not have to be a frightening search; it does not have to be a neurotic or fruitless search. It can be very fruitful. Searching and learning can be synonymous."

"For most people life is a deep pain in the ass," Walter said, "and they stick it behind them and try not to face it."

"Facing it," Terry said, "is a part of the freedom process. Letting the heart and the mind and the soul let go of the world's pain, so the world's pain will not become one's own pain."

He took his hand out of his pocket to light a cigarette, and even though his excitement of the flesh had somewhat subsided, my glance saw a clear outline of what I was determind to have. He must have felt the warmth of my glance. He sat his empty cocktail glass down and held his cigarette in his hand. His left hand went back into his pocket – for the sake of discretion.

I swallowed. I clenched my buttocks. My eyes watered. I tried to control my dreams, but my dreams fell down into his pocket, and he held my dreams in his hand.

I sensed the throbbing of my dreams.

He was looking at Walter and Vera while he was talking to us, but when his eyes came my way, he gave them to me with such a penetrating gaze I could feel the warmth of those exquisitely green emeralds melting and streaming down my throat as though they were a liqueur. Fortunately, I suppose for both of us, he directed his eyes primarily upon Walter and Vera – we could not stand the connection of our eyes for long without the connection of our bodies. That must have been why he did not shake hands when we were introduced, one of us would have drawn the other into our arms.

Yes, there are those times when the communication of feelings, communicated by the untouched flesh, transmits a painful mutual yearning more clearly than words of speech.

14

These words of flesh speak with roaring silence, and there is a drumming of the heart and a drumming of the genitals. And I think of 'That Old Black Magic' and I think of 'Begin the Beguine'. And I want the party to end, but Walter is being so intellectual I could ram my foot a long way up there between his buttocks.

"All this you are saying, I respect, I like, I admire, but if it is not transposed into literature, what happens to it? Where does the spoken word go if it is not written or recorded?"

"It goes into life," Terry Lane said. "It goes into the existence of itself."

"I like that," Vera said. "Don't you like that, Walter? Don't you agree?"

"Of course I like it. Of course I agree. But it doesn't go far enough or deep enough. Time takes it away unless it is put into the written word."

"Oh, but Walter," Vera was saying, and I knew in her heart she was crying, "it doesn't have to be written. It just has to be lived."

(I could imagine Walter sticking his penis between the pages of a book – one by Gide or Proust – and having sex with literature and leaving his fluid there to stick the pages together as he tried to get the pieces of his life stuck together. Poor Walter. Such a brilliant mind, but with only bits and pieces of life.)

"Life without purpose is too shallow," Walter insisted.

I never knew a man more bullheaded than Walter, except for my father who was a Southern clodhopper, as opposite from Walter as any two men can be.

"The purpose of life is life itself. *Living*," Terry insisted.

"Oh, Walter, I know what he means. Don't you?" Vera was in reality begging Walter to love her as much as he loved literature, but she begged like a lady, a lady willing to give. That husband of hers! He felt more pleasure sinking himself into a book than he felt sinking himself into her. And she knew it.

We all have our little touches of hell. Vera's hell was a polite hell – it never exploded, it simply quietly yearned.

Surely there was no hell in Terry Lane's life. He was too beautiful. His emerald-like eyes would have caused the devil

15

himself to melt away or turn-tail and run. I felt more and more as if I were being hypnotized. I did not know if this hypnotism was caused by his quick but piercingly deep occasional gaze, or if it was caused by the blood in his veins, caressing my imagination, or was this the hypnotism of lust? And was this gay lust a prelude to gay love?

I was in a state of overly contained ecstasy, and the containment was stifling my mind as too much smoke in a smoke filled room will stifle the lungs. I wanted the fresh air of open arms closing in upon me. I wanted my heart to stroll in the open meadows of tender caresses. I wanted lips, my tongue, my mouth to drink in the moonbeams of naked night. I wanted the stars to play in my eyes and dance on my forehead and laugh round my skull.

His glances told me that something like this would happen, was bound to happen.

Thank God, he said "No" when someone asked him if he wanted another cocktail.

When would he, when could we, break away from Walter and Vera and the party? It was a wonderful party and I adored Walter and Vera (or did I?), but to hell with it all. I wanted to be alone with Terry Lane.

I desperately wanted another cocktail, but I was afraid, when someone asked me, that if I had another drink Terry would think I was deliberately delaying our departure.

But it was Walter's intellectual expostulations that held us back:

"I know what life is," Walter was insisting more to himself than to anyone else. "But art, all the arts, especially the art of literature, art is the emphasis of life. Art surpasses life, simply because it can and does record it and preserve it, and gives to it posterity. And that is what art it – *giving*. Art is love."

"But isn't love an art?" I managed to interject.

"Yes, it most definitely is," Terry said, and there was just the touch of a smile on his lips, as though he had tasted my words and would save the words for later and swallow the meaning of the words.

"Yes. Yes." Vera merely whispered. She sipped her cocktail. Her glance went round the edge of the cocktail glass.

16

"The play *Romeo and Juliet* certainly has outlived that boy and that girl, and even the one who created them," Walter said defiantly, as though he were proving his point. "The play is more important than the boy and girl in real, so-called *real* life."

"Is the play more important than Shakespeare?" Vera asked.

"That's a good question," Terry said.

"I hate to admit you are sticking me there, but I stick to my point. Human beings are frivolous. Without art they die away and fade. Art is the preservation of humanity."

I was becoming impatient. "Walter, do you remember that verse in the Bible: 'live today for tomorrow ye may die'?"

"Of course. Live. Live. But it all slips away unless the artist catches it."

"You may not realize it," Terry said, "but your philosophy of life and literature is comparable to those fervent religious believers who believe that the seed of a man is for reproductive purposes only."

"That's taking preservation too far," Walter said.

(Walter and Vera did not have any children.)

"Life is meant to be lived, lived for its own sake," I insisted. Then softly I said to Terry, "So let's live it."

"Whatever you say," he agreed. And then to Walter, "I've enjoyed talking with you, even though I disagree with practically everything you have to say. Take care, Vera. Take care."

"I'll call you," I said to Walter and Vera.

And just like that Terry and I walked away.

My head did not seem connected with my body. My head was swirling in a cloud of desire. My heart was pounding with more than desire, only I would not call it more, I would not name this feeling, I was not in the mood for love, I was simply emphatically overwhelmingly in the mood for lust and all its intimate ramifications.

When we were out on the street, Terry removed his hand from his pocket and let the bulge bulge to its heart's content. (Yes, I have often thought the penis has a heart and a mind of its own – it obviously has a head of its own, so why not a heart and a mind? That delightfully uncontrollable part of me has made many a demand on the rest of my life, causing this head on my shoulders to obey, bow down to, even subjugate itself-myself to the head of the rod.)

"I couldn't hold it down any longer," Terry said, and there was a green fire in his eyes, and heavy eagerness in his tone of voice.

"I like what I see, Terry. I love it."

"It's yours."

"You're beautiful."

"Where in God's name do you live?"

"Cross town on the West Side."

"Let's take a cab, but don't sit too close to me. I might lose control. We mustn't upset the cab driver. He might want to join us. I just want you."

Chapter 3

I WANT YOU...

Three of the most beautiful words in the English language. My God, dear Jesus! All the heavens exploded.

How did we undress so quickly? We started undressing in the foyer of my apartment. No, actually we began unloosening our ties in the elevator, unbuttoning our jackets. We started removing our jackets in the foyer, but before we could get them off, we were in each other's arms. We were magnetically forced together by the internal force of desire for each other.

Our lips our tongues our mouths...

Thank God, God created mankind!

Our hands roamed and explored, and we were as intrigued as if this were the first time we had ever touched another body. Buttocks chests genitals cheeks hair...

The kiss would not break. I spoke through his lips.

"The bedroom. Yonder."

He was unbuttoning my shirt. I was unbuttoning his shirt. We were not wearing undershirts. His hand found the naked pap over my heart, and then his lips, his mouth fastened upon the pounding pap.

"Terry. My God, Terry. Terry, let's go to bed."

He faced me, and the emeralds of his eyes swam in the beauty of consent, the beauty of giving, the beauty of sharing. We did not break the embrace; it was something of a gliding dance, our getting from the foyer into the living room. Then we paused again, our hands roamed again. Our lips kissed their way from lips to cheeks to eyelids and to the lips again. Our passions were forcing us to become each other. Somehow our jackets had fallen on the floor, somehow our

19

shirts had fallen. We were barechested. Neither of us were muscular; neither of us were hairy. We were enchanted, one by the other. My lips went from one of his paps to the other. I wished that I had been born as Siamese twins so that I could take them both simultaneously.

I tried to speak but my vocal chords did not want to work. Then I forced the words out: "The bedroom. Through that door." But even as I said the words, I sank to my knees and I kissed his crotch, and was vaguely aware that he was wearing grey flannel trousers.

"Wait," he said.

He started to lift me but instead he fell down beside me. His mouth grabbed my mouth as though he were a hungry starving man.

Then we seemed to be lifting each other up, loosening each other's belts. There had been a bedspread on the bed, but somehow our hands – one of his, one of mine – reached out and it was on the floor. We lowered each other's trousers and the protruding maleness of ourselves made his shorts and my briefs slightly difficult to remove.

And we were naked.

We paused.

Our trousers and our underwear were around our ankles. Our shoes and socks were still on. But we had to pause and gaze. Like many lovers before us, we created our own Garden of Eden in a bedroom in Manhattan, but we were not aware of the existence of anyone in this entire big swirling world. We were alone. We were the uniqueness of ourselves. Quietly, as though the beauty of our nakedness had stunned us and caused the intensity to recede momentarily inside ourselves, quietly we sat on the edge of the bed and removed our shoes, our trousers, our underwear, our socks, while our eyes were still on the uplifted nakedness of ourselves, the magical flesh of ourselves.

We left our things on the floor on the side of the bed.

Slowly now our arms reached out and we embraced as we rolled onto the bed on our sides, simply sinking our eyes into the eyes of the other. The purity of the green his eyes. The unshed tears of joy, bliss in my eyes. We mirrored our souls in the eyes of one another. We did not think about it, but surely we knew, surely we felt: we were created in the image of God.

During these moments, we deified each other.

We were the gods of each other.

He gave me his lips and I gave him my lips and the tenderness of this kiss lasted on and on until we could no longer be tender and it became fiercely strong and we were animalizing ourselves even as we were in the act of deification, giving ourselves to the magnificence of each other.

He turned me on my back and he covered me: he covered me with softness and tenderness and hardness, and his mouth was my mouth, and my tongue was his tongue.

His mouth tried to leave my mouth. It went to my throat, but was drawn back again. Then I felt his tongue on my throat again. Then his head, his face, his lips were going from one of my paps to the other. My mind drifted into a haze of delights, the haze of ecstasy. His tongue explored my belly. And my heart screamed silently as he sank his lips down to the root of my stalk and softly he rubbed his nose in my pubic hair and then up to the head of my stalk again. "Not yet," and quickly his face came to my face again and I sucked his tongue.

The intermingling of two men, the merging and re-merging of two separate entities into seemingly one, the union of bliss and ecstasy, this, these acts of pre-love, this is the creation of divinity in one another; this is the earthiness of sheer heaven. The power of passion, the turbulence of youth. The demands of the flesh – flesh created in the image of God. The earth of ourselves. I could feel my God swirling down on me and waving sheets of heaven all around us.

We were pure in the purity of our passions; we were free from sin for I was free from the olden gods of punishment I had been taught in my childhood in the South. We were cleansed of social evils, for we gave freely of the goodness of ourselves. We pleased God in pleasing ourselves. We worshipped, idolized, the God within, for it is true as it is written : "God is within."

We were blessed with each other.

And I felt the heaven of ourselves with each touch he gave

21

me, and I had cause to believe he was feeling the same heaven from me within himself.

He slid himself down in the bed and his tongue trailed along my flesh, and he tasted the moisture on the head of my stalk and his tongue slid down the underside of this staff of bliss, and this tongue of a thousand delights touched upon my root and I felt him lifting my legs as though they were the wings of a butterfly and his mighty tongue sought the depths between my buttocks, and he soul kissed me between my buttocks and I felt my spirit melting into a quiet form of lightning, and the probing of his tongue caused my belly to sink and I moved as though I were on the waters of a Holy Sea and my unidentified dreams were walking upon the waters, and I knew, in time, he would change the waters not into wine, but into the very cream of ourselves.

And then his tongue was at my lips again and the rod of himself was entering me, sinking into me, and my breath breathed him into me, and the hairs around that incredible implement mingled with the hairs around the hole of myself, and I tightened and untightened my buttocks, and he whispered, barely audibly: "Never like this. It's never been like this." I felt the words on my lips, words from his mouth in my mouth. And then something happened to me that had truly never happened before: while still locked between the intimate flesh of my buttocks, his lips travelled down my body and he lifted me in such a way that my staff entered the ruby gates of his lips and he was doing me as he was simultaneously probing into the depths of me.

And it was almost more than I could bear.

Yet I bore it.

My arms reached up toward the ceiling toward the sky, and then they fell and my fingers caressed the hairs of his head. Then my arms lifted again and I wanted to fly with the angels in heaven because this was a paradise over and beyond any paradise I had ever known.

He was the creation and consummation of dreams with each movement of his body in my body while my staff of paradise was in the paradise of his moist and divinely hungry mouth.

He was a man within a man.

We were as God created us to be.

We did not invent ourselves – we simply gave vent to ourselves in the exuberance of our flesh as our flesh commands us in the reality of this our nature.

As the roots of a tree enters the earth and the tree grows, so grew our nature.

As one stream flows into another stream, we were flowing into each other.

As night follows day and day follows night, we followed our nature.

We were as imperfect as a rocky field, yet we were as divine as the very heavens themselves.

We were so very human.

We were as old as Greek history, probably older, yet we are born again and again.

Our seed gives birth to new moments of ecstasy, and though the seed may fade away, they shall be born again and again.

Neither famine nor disease nor laws shall wipe us from the face of the earth, for we are in the nature of nature itself.

Man must love man.

This is the mirror of divine justice.

"Terry, Terry," my whispers fell from my lips while his lips worked upon the magic of my flesh, for all my life I have believed this lifting of our flesh to be a magical thing.

Now I was feeling the intensity of his bodily-heavenly movements deep within the gates of my buttocks.

His hunger became ravenous.

He was an-animal-a-god-a-man, all in one. He was tender in the strength of himself, a tamed wildness.

A man inside a man.

And now the prelude to the orgasms of ourselves was beginning, and the prelude gave me a bright blindness, a gasp of heights where the stars bit into me and the moon caressed me as the cream of myself exploded and flowed most generously into the one who was giving me the emphatic cream of himself.

I felt the liquid eruption of him down deep inside me.

I felt him swallowing, drinking the inside of myself.

Now we were deadly quiet in the supreme life of exquisite passion-at-rest.

Thank you, God, for making me gay.
Thank God for the love of man for man.

We were silent. We had to be. We were exhausted in our exhilaration. We had travelled from the earth to paradise and back again. He withdrew slowly. I was clean, and he was clean. For a while, he rested his head on my belly. My fingers rested in his blond hair. We savoured the aftermath. We tasted the quiet.

We knew, without voicing it, we knew that this was not ordinary sex. Ordinary sex was a once or twice a week happening with a stranger or a casual acquaintance. We had gone far beyond bargain basement sex.

We had been transported.

We had fallen in love.

He was the first to name it, he was the first to discover it: "We love each other," he spoke quietly; the breath of his words touched my belly.

For a moment my hand was still.

Then I said, almost protestingly, "I was not ready to love again."

And still very quietly he spoke: "But you do. You love me. You don't have to be ready. You love me whether you want to or not. We did not merely have sex, we made love. Something inside ourselves made us fall in love.

"It wasn't just sex," I agreed. "I know that. I can turn away or walk away from others with the greatest of ease. You gave me such a part of yourself, it was like, it's like, when you were coming inside me, a part of your soul was coming inside me. And I believe I felt my soul coming inside you."

"Maybe that is the real wedding of two men, souls coming inside each other."

When he said the word "wedding", his wife came into my mind, but just as quickly, I put her out again. I had no room for her inside my head. She would have caused a tumult there. Now we were at peace, *a peace beyond understanding, peace that surpasseth all understanding.*

The beauty in the purity of naked love gave us this peace. We were stripped of the world. For a little while. The world did not exist.

We were Adam and Adam in the Garden of Eden.

There was no serpent in my bedroom, no serpent in my Garden. (At least, not yet, God. Keep the outside world out. Free us from the social blunders of life. Free us from the evils of society.)

We are pure in the purity of ourselves. We are pure in the naked souls of ourselves.

We mirror the flesh of one another.

We mirror the souls of one another, and drink in the differences along with the liquid mirror.

"Terry," I paused. "Say it."

His lips touched my belly lightly. And he spoke into the depths of my belly, "I love you, Phillip."

"You love me." There was wonderment in the tone of my voice.

"Yes."

"I love you, too."

We were so quiet as we spoke, as we declared our love for each other, we might have heard the falling of feathers from the wings of angels falling down all around us.

We were beyond reality. We were the consummation of dreams dreamed by all the lonely men dreaming through a thousand years, searching for the love of their dreams, searching through the years, searching through hearts and bodies and souls. Searching through tears fallen unseen, or dropped in an empty cocktail glass.

I said it again. I wanted to hear it again. "I love you, Terry. I love you."

"Phillip…"

My name on his lips, lips on my belly.

And then: "Phillip." He spoke my name into my pubic hair.

Then he brought his body up, and he lightly covered me. His eyes gazed into my eyes. I felt as if I were gazing into his soul, and I believe he sensed something in my soul that no other man had ever sensed. The true divinity of love. No deeper love I had ever known. And I could feel the incomparable depths of his love.

He kissed me softly, tenderly, as though he were touching the heart of a bird. He kissed each of my eyelids as if velvet were touching velvet. His emerald eyes gazed into my hazel eyes. He saw my heart and soul. He breathed upon me and with me. No priest, preacher or rabbi could have joined us together more sacredly. No judge could do for us what we had done for ourselves and were doing. We were beyond the law. We were, we are, the law of nature. Our birthrights bled into our souls, and we were, we are, born into a love that crowns the kingdom of supreme flesh. He pressed himself close to me and worked his arms under me, and he kissed my open lips with his open lips and our tongues roamed into the red-darkness of our mouths and the suction of our mouths intensified as the moments fell into memories, memories that would fall, years later, onto the pages of a manuscript to be written down as they are, indeed, written down and give me back again the most beautiful love of my long life, even now in memory it is as if I feel again as I felt in reality then, the growing of his long staff. Staffs of life, staffs of passion, staffs of love. The magic staff of Moses was no more magic than the divine rods of ourselves. Love is always a miracle.

The moments lingered. The magic lingered.

Our kisses delayed ourselves until we could no longer control the return of our intimate desires. "Let me do you first," I said. "You've had mine, now let me have yours. I'm hungry for you."

He turned me over on his back, and my hand felt and held his uplifted dream-flesh, while my tongue tasted his throat and each of his paps, even as his tongue had known me previously, and then my tongue went to his belly, but I could not linger there. The superb meat of him was throbbing for me, just as if there were a heart filled with overflowing love, love in his penis itself. It was only then, strangely, that I noticed there were flecks of gold in his blond pubic hair, truly I had found a gold mine of desire.

I filled my hunger with the world's most intimate food, and heaven came down to me while invisible angels sang quietly in our blood and waltzed in the air around us. We were the gods of ourselves, and God Himself did not close His eyes to us or turn form us.

My hands caressed this flesh of cream while my throat was being caressed by his magic rod of dreams. I worked my hand under his buttocks and I felt the silk hairs around his asshole, a hole for my tongue, a hole that my staff of pleasure would some time delve into. But not now. My erotic mouth was feasting upon the flesh of heaven, this most intimate miracle of man – the lifting of itself, the resurrection of the flesh, the creaming of itself.

"Not yet," he said. "I'll make it last."

He took my head in his hands, and lifting himself up from the waist, he brought his lips to my lips and he sucked my tongue.

"My God," he whispered. "It's almost like sucking myself, sucking your tongue that's just been sucking me only seconds ago." And he drew my tongue into his mouth again. He let go of me, sank back down onto the bed, and my mouth sank down to the root of his passions.

Surely this dream will be with me all the days and all the nights of my life.

These words did not come to me as spoken words or transposed words from the Scriptures. They came to me as a feeling in my blood and they roamed through my veins and they have lived with me either consciously or subconsciously through many a year of my life. And the feeling is only now being put into the written word, held here on these pages, as I have held the memory-dream, the dream-memory, all these many years in my heart and soul.

This youth of ours, this youth that remains in the world of my dreams and in the world of my memory as young as it was when I was twenty-three and he was twenty-seven.

I could feel his pleasure in my pleasure. His was not merely a pleasure in the genitals, this feeling surged throughout his body; and this tasting of the miraculous rod of him not only in my mouth and my throat, it penetrated my heart and my mind and touched every part of me. My lungs breathed his rod as I sucked upon this luxurious velvet of meat.

There is no luxury more supremely rich than the luxury of intimacy.

Now I could feel the cream of his internal body building up in him, and my eyes were burning with the stars and my heart became a pounding moon for the two of us. And so there came from deep inside of him this magic liquid fire of silver, and my mouth was filled to almost overflowing, but I would not give waste to a drop of these dreams – I swallowed down into the depths of myself that which had come from the depths of him.

It was as though he lined my insides with the fluid of himself, even as a coat is lined with cream-coloured satin, I was internally lined with liquid satin.

I held a part of it in my mouth and rolled it around inside my mouth before I let it slide down my throat and into the depths of me.

I could not let go.

He had to gently lift my head, and remove his penis and hold one hand over his genitals, and I kissed the back of that restraining hand.

I breathed into my lungs the golden flecks of his blond pubic hair.

My eyelids played with the stars he had given to my eyes.

I lifted my head.

"Come to me," he said. "To my lips."

I drew my body up, and hazily our glances met, and we met in the heart of ourselves, our lips tenderly met, softly, softly we gave and we received our kisses of contentment. Each kiss said *Thank you for the supremacy of the moment*.

Now the miracle of time is this: that moment has lingered with me for close on to forty years, all the moments of that beautiful evening, that beautiful night, that first time with the most beautiful man of my life.

I was limp in these moments of aftermath, a time when we lovers float in a mist of ourselves, as though we are drifting in space on tender blue and white clouds. Softly and tenderly caressing one another, sometimes with only the little finger of his hand on my hand.

Time forgetting to move, time being tucked away in a chest of drawers, undisturbed beneath an old pair of underwear. Time disassociated with the world of ordinary life and existence.

And then he moved one of his legs in such a way that it brushed against my limp, and the limp began to grow and move of itself. We had been on our sides, he on his left, me on my right; now he drew me over on top of him. I could sense the way he wanted me. I lifted my buttocks and pressed the growing erection of myself against his golden-flecked pubic hair, and my lips pressed intensely against his lips; his arms encircled me; my hands went down his sides; my tongue parted his lips and he slightly opened his mouth as my tongue wedged itself into a mositure of splendid paradise. My buttocks lifted, then slowly pressured down, again, then again.

He sucked upon my tongue till I felt tears in my eyes, and then his tongue pushed my tongue out of his mouth as he whispered upon my lips, "Phillip, Phillip, soul-kiss me between my buttocks. Then sink yourself down deep inside me."

mouth, the tongue that had spoken such intimate words, this I did before I let my face caress his chest, his waist, his belly, and lick the semi-limpness of his divine rod.

He drew his legs up, then each of his hands clasped himself underneath his knees and he drew his lower self higher, till my face was between his beautiful buttocks, and his hands split his cheeks wider as I soul-kissed his asshole, probingly, unable to press hardly a quarter of an inch of my tongue into the exquisitely personal flesh of him, longing, pressing, yearning to make a penis of my tongue; then circling the circle of his anus with my hungry tongue, then stiffening and flattening, stiffening and flattening my tongue with as much pressure upon his anus as I could muster.

"God... God... God..." I was vaguely aware of this passionate prayer from his lips, as if he were making a god of me, yet he was not forsaking his God – he was, we were, merging the godliness of ourselves with the Almighty God in the power, through the power, of supreme intimacy.

The suction of my mouth drew the meat of his ass slightly into my mouth while my tongue probed at the hole of his ass.

"Easy. Easy, Phillip, easy."

My mouth released my hold upon him and I licked his ass soothingly.

"Now do that again, Phillip. Do it again the way you were when I had to stop you. Just the same way."

And so I did, and I held onto him until he again in exquisite non-pain-pain had to stop me, and he said beggingly, as a beggar begging for a rainbow: "Take me, Phillip. Put it inside me, Phillip. Give it to me."

And so I lifted my head and I lifted my body up and over him, and the staff of my growing love for him was moist in its yearning, and I slid this staff of my manliness into, slowly into, the reddish-brown depths of him, even down to the root of myself, and as I heard a gasp of ecstasy come from his mouth, my lips sank to his lips, and the movements of myself in him was as a personal sea upon the rounded shores of earthly-flesh.

I felt as if I was giving every part of myself to him, not only my staff of eight glorious inches, but every ounce of my flesh, every drop of my blood, every beat of my heart, every thought of my mind.

This was a union of dreams.

This was as if one lonely moon had wandered through space, delving into ordinary heavenly delights, until it came upon another moon who had known the world and parts and places of heaven, and the two moons meet, they touch, and they are born again into the purity of experience beyond all the experiences theretofore known in heaven or on earth. And the two moons grow so close to one another, they merge and they are the one moon, united in the bliss of heaven and flesh, waking dreams never before dreamed and creating stars till then unknown.

Thus the incredibility of miracles becomes man's union with man.

And the incredibility of God is that He gave Himself to us in the image of Himself, and that we are the gods of earthly delights while sparks of heaven flash through us, and surely this coming of myself came from my very heart and I emptied my soul into him, even as my soul expanded and grew within itself.

This fluid from within myself became his.

We became a mixture of one another.

Chapter 4

AFTER THAT SUPREME mixture only a little time passed, maybe twenty minutes or so, when he sat up in bed and said, "I'm sorry, but I have to go."

"But why?" I was a little shocked. I did not want him to go.

"I'm married. You know that. I saw you looking at the ring on my finger."

His back was to me.

"Thank you for making me forget it. For a little while," I said as I gazed at the smoothness of his back.

"I can forget it, too. For a little while."

"You belong to her," I sighed, regretfully.

"I belong to myself. Now you have become a part of me, myself, the self I want to share with you," and on these words he turned and faced me. He gathered me up into his arms, as though he were lifting up the contents of a treasure chest, and he said, "Please don't hold my marriage against me. We can work it out, if we can be patient." He kissed me, he pleaded, "Please be patient. I have fallen in love with you."

"I'll be patient," I promised. "I'm not sure how you mean that. But I'll be patient."

"Will you let me see you next Sunday afternoon. No cocktail party. No time with others. Just the two of us. All afternoon and all evening. Your body in my arms telling me you will. Let me hear you say it."

"Yes. Yes. Of course I will. Do you want to meet me here, or somewhere else first?"

"Here. Alone with you. No one else."

"I'll write down my address for you before you go."

"No need to. I'll remember it forever."

Then quickly he kissed me on my genitals, and dashed from the bed. "Where are my clothes?"

"Scattered everywhere."

We laughed as we gathered up his things. Our laughter was not free laughter. It was slightly strained. I was wondering, "Does he really mean what he says? Will he be here again next Sunday?" And later I learned that he was wondering, "Will he be patient with me? Or will he hold my marriage against me?"

I watched him dress. I liked watching him. I did not like seeing him getting ready to go. Yet I liked watching him. His shoes and socks, trousers and underwear were here in the bedroom. First, he put on his shorts, covering the most intimate areas of himself. That seemed to wake me; it jarred me out of a hazy dream, a blinding dream of rainbows plunging through his heart and into mine. Then he stepped into his trousers and buttoned the top button. He sat on the side of the bed and began to put on his socks and his shoes. I kissed his bare back, softly touching it. "Don't," he said. "If you don't stop, I'll have to turn round and take you in my arms again and make love to you. Please don't. I should have left an hour ago. Your touch goes all through me."

Those last words were spoken almost painfully, as though he were grinding them out of his throat. He moved quickly to a nearby chair, taking his shoes and socks with him. I propped myself on my elbow; I could not take my eyes off him.

His socks were on. He was putting on his shoes. He was tying his shoe laces. He spoke: "I feel your eyes undressing me while I am getting dressed. You have too much magnetism."

"I'm not going to squelch it," I said. "I can't."

"I don't want you to squelch it. I simply have to make my duty be stronger than my desire. Even stronger than my love."

I did not ask him this, but I was wondering: Is duty stronger than love? Does it have to be? Why? Why should anything be stronger than love?

Later we discussed this, and I was hurt when I first learned the answer to that question. And I knew that everyone does not, cannot, have the same answer. Yet each answer is correct.

The heart becomes a questionnaire when a new lover is ready to go.

"I feel your love. You're over there in the chair. I'm here on the bed. But I feel your love touching me."

"I want my love to touch you no matter where I am, no matter where we are. While I am on the subway train going home to my family, I want my love to be touching you."

I did not ask him, but I wondered: "Will you be touching me while you are making love to your wife? While you are inside her, will you remember being inside me? Will you remember me being inside you?"

I wondered these things, and I knew it would be cruel to ask those questions now. It was even cruel to myself, I suppose, to be thinking these questions of his other life.

His other life...

He had known her for years. They had a son five years old and another four. He had been making love to her – how often? – once or twice, two or three times a week, for all those years.

He had known me for only one night, not even a full night. Just this one evening.

Yet it was an evening that surpassed all other evenings in my life. Could he be feeling the same? His actions, his reactions, indicated that for him, too, this was a time like no other time that life and time had ever given us. We had gone beyond all other experiences in coming into each other's arms.

She had the time and the children.

Perhaps I had the supremacy.

Perhaps.

He was fully dressed. He stood still for a moment. For that moment we did not speak. He gazed at me. I was still stretched out on the bed, naked, propped on one elbow. His emerald eyes gazed into my eyes; touched, without touching, my lips. He looked at my chest as though he were reading the contents of my heart. He must have read the pulsations of love. Then his glance fell upon my genitals, quickly, then back to my eyes again.

"I can't kiss you goodnight," he said. "Forgive me. I simply can't. If I do, I'll make love to you again. Don't get up. I'll let myself out. I'll be starving until next Sunday."

He turned and went on his way toward a way of life entirely different from my way of life, this way he had shared with me.

Children.

Thank God, I had no children.

A wife.

God forbid.

A home filled with love… That created a different picture in my mind.

Imagine… not being alone. So much of the time alone. Aloneness was a part of me, too much of me. Yes, I had long ago wiped out of my life any idea of family. My own home life, while I was growing up, was not a home of love. There were too many quarrels, demands, orders, nagging, tears.

As an early teenager I began thinking about getting away from all that. At nineteen I escaped from the emotional prison of homelife. I quickly grasped and held onto that old saying: *home is where the heart is.*

Now I must admit my love, this philosophical heart, wandered around quite a bit, from furnished room to furnished room, from man to man. I lived in a world of searching men, men finding the beauty of nakedness and the sorrows of goodbye; men making promises and men breaking promises. Promiscuity was in high fashion. I loved it. Yet my heart contradicted my body and my lips and sought one true love.

Just one, my soul prayed.

Just one, my heart pleaded.

Yet my blood flowed wildly through my veins from bar to bar, the baths, the men's rooms in the subways, Woolworth's on Fifth Avenue in the basement, anywhere there was action, darkened corners of movie houses; oh, how wild my blood was in the heat of strangers who were as wild as myself.

How many times, while in the arms of a stranger, I had asked myself: will this be a real love, will this be a true love?

Somehow with Terry, I did not ask myself. Somehow I knew. We seemed to have melted into each other. The fluid

34

from my body, which he had taken into himself, I sensed, I believed, my fluid had lined his heart and his soul, even as his fluid, created from deep within his vital organs, had lined my heart and soul.

It was as though our seed, not entering the womb of a woman but entering each other, did beget and conceive a love beyond the womb of woman. Our hearts were wombs turned masculine.

How could I live without him all that time till next Sunday? Then I asked myself: how did I live without him all that time till I met him?

I lived in the search; I lived in the dream; I lived in a world of false love, fleeting episodes. Flesh for flesh; pleasure for pleasure. Lust personified. And much of it was good, damn good! In memory, I praise myself for all the good times of my life, those remembered, those forgotten.

Yet, these things, these times, are different from the time of love for there is something godly about love, and it is written in the Holy Scriptures: God is love. Oh, that is open to many interpretations and each may interpret in his own way. But I interpret it to mean that when lovers love, whoever the lovers may be, God gives a touch of His infinitesimal self to the lovers, and some part of Him, a breath of Him, becomes a part of the lovers; thus it is true... God is love.

He gave us His blessings because we gave so much to each other.

God does not discriminate, nor does He look down with scorn, for we are His creation as surely as the roots of a tree, as surely as the lilies of the valley, yes, all these things, all; we exist through His divine will.

We are the roots of love; we are the flowers of love.

Our impurities are the impurities of the world.

We are clean in the eyes of God; we are clean in the eyes of love.

We are God's will.

Chapter 5

THE NEXT DAY Walter called me. I knew he would. His repressed homosexuality thrived on the activities of others.

I had heard him say a hundred times or more, "Oh, I know what it's like. When I was fourteen, this guy and I, we, oh, we carried on." He did not say just how they carried on, but bubbles came into the corners his mouth, so I assumed the bubbles were dreaming in retrospect. "But of course that way of life turned out not to be for me. Year of two later I met a girl. Loose is what they called them back in those days. Real loose. We got together every Saturday night after the movies in her backyard, on the grass, in the shadow of the hedges. That's all we cared about. Being in the shadow of those hedges. We'd sit squirming through the movie, and we'd always watch it all the way through, not caring two cents about it, because she said it'd be indecent to leave early. That would mean we were nothing better than pigs about the flesh. People who carried on, she let me know plain and simple, such people who carried on without doing something else first were the low down type. If they went to the movies or to church – she later became a Sunday school teacher – or went to a dance or went visiting each other's folks, that proved they didn't have a one track mind. People with one track minds were nobodies. And I guess she's proved her point to herself. She's not thirty yet and she's living with her third husband.

"But back then, neither one of us had any thought of getting married. 'I don't do this cause I'm bad,' she said. 'I do this cause when I get married, I don't want to be a flop for my husband. I want to learn something for his sake. But when I get myself a husband, I'll pretend he's teaching me everything I know, cause I know husbands like to teach wives that. Why I heard one of my mother's friends a-talking to my mother, telling her how she made her first husband believe she was a virgin. She took a rubber and put just a little ketchup in it. And she moaned like it was her first time. And while he was a-going away at it, half out of his mind; his head in another world mind you, she just emptied the contents of that rubber underneath her rump on the bedsheets, then tucked the empty rubber under the edge of the mattress, and that rascal never knowed no difference.

"I plan to do the same when I get married. If a woman don't fool a man she's bound to make a fool of herself instead. But I'll be hanged if I'm going to give my future husband a dumb bride.' And on that score she lived up to her word.

"So everybody has their own interpretations of what is the best thing to do. I didn't lie to Vera. A man doesn't have to lie. That guy, that once. Vera had read Oscar Wilde and she loved his work. Then when she heard about his personal life, I guess she sort of forgave him. Anyway, when we were engaged she made me promise not to let another male fool around with me. (Did she remember to get him to promise not to fool around with another man?) And then I told her about the girl in the shadow of the hedges, and she said such things were to be expected of a man. And in those days, a woman was expected to be a virgin till her wedding night. And she was. I can smell the difference in ketchup and blood. I guess if a guy can't it's because his mind is too carried away. Of course she made me promise not to look at another woman. She knows I look but that's all I do. That's only natural."

Walter did not admit that he also looked at other men, not just in the eye – he often avoided eye-contact – but he looked below the waist. More than once I had felt Walter's eyes upon my crotch. And if eyes could burn, my trousers would have gone up in flame.

I do not know if Vera was aware of his glances. I assume she was vaguely conscious of the direction of his eyes, but I do not believe she let herself believe he had any homosexual desires, consciously or subconsciously. Vera could not deal with confrontations. She blanked half of life out of her mind.

(I'm not saying there have been times in my own life when I have seen and felt things much too clearly, turning a beam of light into a slender sword.) Vera could shrug off anything better than anyone I have ever known.

At that literary cocktail party, I was aware that Walter's eyes had fallen upon Terry's crotch, and I knew that Walter knew why Terry's hand was in his left pocket. Walter's eyes were impregnated with the promiscuity of his glances. But Walter was not as brazen as his eyes. He swallowed down blank desires. He talked around his repressions and he hemmed-and-hawed with his inhibitions. Where did his thoughts go while he was making love to his wife? I had an idea that his thoughts sometimes centred upon me. Walter was attractive, tall and innocently gawky. Maybe I would have desired him if I had known him for a while before I met Vera, but Vera seemed to be a part of him, so much a part of Walter that I could not desire him.

I did not know Terry's wife. At this point, I did not even know her name. I knew she existed, but she did not seem to be a part of Terry. Terry, even after only one evening, seemed to be a part of me. His wife was something dangling out there in the distance, hanging somewhere in space. Something like a shirt hanging on a clothesline, not even a pair of shorts, just a shirt hanging out there somewhere to dry in the wind, not even the sunshine, certainly not the moonlight, just hanging in the wind.

(Would the shirt blow away?)

Whatever she was – wife, leftover love, mother, duty – she had enough drawing power to cause him to get up out of my bed and go home to her.

"Interesting guy we met at that cocktail party," Walter said, and his tone of voice said: tell me what happened, titillate me with the naked details.

"He is more than interesting," I said.

"Yeah?" He paused. "Well, you fellows didn't go to another party, did you?" Meaning, did you go home to bed?

"It was better than any party. It was better than anything that ever happened in my life?"

"My God," he said, "sounds like, sounds like you enjoyed yourself."

"It was more than that. It was more than anything. Words can only go so far. Words can only say so much."

"But you are a man of words. You know I think you are one of the best writers of our generation."

Walter had told me that after he had read my first published book, and he said it again after reading some of my unpublished stories, but when I realized he was harbouring an inactivated desire for me, I wondered if his desire in any way influenced his opinion of my writings. Yet I realized that repressed desire will just as often, if not more often, turn a straight man against a gay man as it may cause him to seek the gay element in someone. However, after talking with Vera, who felt very much as Walter did about my work, I believe Walter was sincere in his literary opinions. He did not know how to be sincere, meaning honest, in his undercurrent homosexual desires.

Walter walked a phallic tightrope; he yearned and held back; he burned and quenched the fires of his blood or turned the fearful fires over to his wife.

Once I asked Walter, "Do married men ever masturbate?"

"Of course we do. The man who says he doesn't is a liar. It's as natural as scratching. But a strange thing happens when I masturbate. As much as I love Vera, her image doesn't come into my mind."

I paused before asking, "What sort of image does come into your mind?"

He looked away. Not strong enough or brave enough to face the answer, he said, "I'll never tell anyone that. Not even you." Then realizing the implication of his answer, he said, "Oh, you know how it is. All sorts of images. Of course I don't do it much except when Vera's having her period."

I knew I was part of Walter's subconscious life, a part he let out, released from the fly of his mind, only in the semi-darkness of himself. He did not want to turn the light on. Yet he searched for knowledge in other areas of his life. He probed.

"Will you be seeing him again?"

"Yes," I said. "We've promised to see each other again."

"You know he has a wife and two children." Walter tried to make his comment sound casual, but I knew he was wondering how does a married man go about living a double life?

"I know. But I can't, or rather, I won't let myself think about that." Yes, there were areas of my life I had trouble facing, areas I did not want to believe existed. Why was I letting myself fall in love with a man who was already taken? A casual rendezvous was nothing to be concerned about, but the intensity of my feelings were far from casual.

"Oh, it's just a passing thing," Walter commented.

He and Vera had often joked with me about my numerous affairs, most of which did not last long enough to be called affairs. Walter once made the comment that they were simply "intimate eruptions of desire."

"No, Walter. I don't think it's just a passing thing. I think it's the real thing this time."

"I believe I've heard you say that before," he said. He was trying not to be critical.

"I know you have. But this time…" Yes, how often I had said those words before, how often I had felt similar feelings.

But I could not say that I had ever before felt this feeling of such supreme depths.

"Don't let yourself be hurt, and watch out you don't hurt yourself." If Walter had been brave enough and broad enough, he would have been my father and my mother and my lover, but somehow I felt he was a child wandering in the darkness of himself, halfway realizing where the chord was that he could pull to give himself light, but being more afraid of the light than of the darkness or even the semi-darkness, he only touched it – he did not pull the chord. Maybe he had married Vera to help him not pull a chord that fascinated but quietly frightened him.

"People are bound to be hurt sometime or other in their lives, Walter. I don't want to be hurt, but the fear of it is not going to stand in my way. With me, within myself, my dreams are stronger than my fears." (I was not hitting out at him. I was simply revealing there was a difference.) "When I send out a manuscript, I have to believe more in its acceptance than fear its rejection. I won't let my heart be stagnated. I'm in love with Terry. All other loves or thoughts of love were simply building up to this love."

"But you gay people fall in love too fast. That's why the affairs so often fall through." (I could not argue with that.) "You met just yesterday, and here you are on a pink cloud of love today."

"Gay love doesn't fool around – it gets to the point."

"Ha!" He almost laughed. "You've fooled around more than anyone I've ever known."

"That's a different kind of fooling around."

But when the fooling around suddenly ceases and you suddenly fall in love, the fall is deep, the intensity springs high, and the self is engulfed with the power of gay love.

"Sometimes, Phillip, I think when your body fools around and, and, and other areas of your desire (he meant my oral desires), I think you are safer than when you let yourself get emotionally involved."

I did not realize that Walter had paid that much attention to my emotions.

"The flesh is safer than the emotions. The flesh is easier to deal with. But when I love, I love! I don't know how to put a harness on my emotions. I give myself to the one I love."

"I don't want you to be offended when I say this," Walter spoke cautiously, "but you are more emotional than a woman."

"I'm not offended. I admit to being too emotional. But I prefer to think that I am more free with my emotions than most straight men and possibly more honest than some women. (Vera was in almost straightlaced control of her emotions. I believe he was comparing me with his wife, but I don't think he knew that.) But I'd rather," I spoke seriously, "be free with my emotions than tied up inside myself, afraid to face my feelings, afraid to reveal to my feelings."

"Yes. Yes." Walter spoke slowly. He might have been hearing words from a mirror – did he ever dare look beneath his shaving cream while he was shaving around his lips, or while he was shaving his throat? "I suppose it's better to face up, but a man has to be careful about what he faces up to."

"I think everyone needs to be careful about whatever we do. But there is a difference in being careful and fearful. If we take our feelings too far we are simply covering up another feeling."

And I took care not to say too much. I did not want to encourage Walter to "come out." I don't think he would have known how to deal with being actively gay. It might have driven him out of his mind. (So I thought then when I was in my early twenties, and he was about thirty.) Also, I believed there was more of the heterosexual in his character than the homosexual. He would have been as confused as blazing hell if he tried to live the life of an active bisexual. As a matter of fact, I did not think Walter was good at anything except being an intellectual, and he was too damned good at that. His mind sucked on literature and philosophy.

"And literature is the place," he expostulated, "for revealing all feelings."

"Literature is a good place," I agreed, "but what about life itself? Life is also a good place for revealing all feelings."

"It simply can't always be. It simply can't, can't always be." He was like a man struggling with a stuck zipper, trying to get it open, but the zipper was on his mind. It is not unusual for a brilliant intellect to be an emotional fool. "Life needs more editing than literature."

"That depends upon whose life you are talking about. I don't want my life edited. That would be too much like censorship."

"No. No," he insisted. "Censorship is deplorable. Editing, editing is an art."

"So long as it is not surgery, I am sure you are right about editing. But I don't want an editor or a politician cutting out my balls or stuffing paper down my heart. I have to have freedom."

"Don't enslave yourself trying to find freedom. This new guy, this new love you claim to have found, try not to be a slave to this free love." He paused. And then I could barely hear him when he said, "He's married."

I wanted to kill him. There was too much truth now to what he was saying. I knew that man was married. I did not need Walter to tell me. I knew my heart could easily make a slave of itself, if I simply let it.

Don't enslave yourself trying to find freedom.

Dear God, if Walter could see himself as clearly as he sometimes saw me, he would, of course, be a different man.

I liked Walter, even when I didn't like him.

Now I wondered if Walter was giving me these warnings for my own sake, out of sheer friendship, or were there elements of jealousy in his feelings toward me? Did he simultaneously desire me and not desire me? There is a wanting and a not-wanting in many men, the mixture of feelings, opposing natures of oneself, the fighting of a dream, and the refusal to resolve the fight and make up to the dream.

I recalled having heard Vera comment about Walter twisting in his sleep, and how she had made herself grow accustomed to his twisting and turning.

There are many sides to any man's nature; the many sides of Walter were simply more obvious to me than they were to himself, and even though Vera may have felt the other sides of his nature, I do not believe she believed what she felt. Not her husband, not Walter. That sort of thing was fascinating in others; that sort of thing was fascinating in literature, but of course it was not in her husband, and if it were, it was only to a 'very normal degree.'

"I'll try not to love him too much," I said. "I'm only too well aware that he's married, but I didn't intend to fall in love with him. It simply happened."

"Does his wife know he's gay?"

"I believe she does. He said he told her everything about himself before he married her."

"He might have meant he told her everything about himself except that. I've never understood how a woman could deal with her husband having sex with another man or another woman."

"I suppose, if she wants him enough, she'll have to share him. I want Terry so much that I am willing to share him with his wife. Especially, damn it, since she got him before I did."

"You're not afraid this will break up their marriage?"

"It could. But I don't think it will. If it does that would be his business, the breaking up. After the break up, then it would be my business to see if I could make him all my own."

"What about the children?"

Again, I could kill Walter. "I don't know. I don't think I want to think about the children."

"I know I'm being nosey," Walter apologized. "But Vera

and I, we just don't want you to be hurt."

He gave me an invitation to have dinner with him and Vera for the following Friday evening. We said good night.

His telephone call had made me think about what I did not want to think about: the reality of Terry Lane's marriage, and the plain truth of the results of that marriage – two sons.

My sexual relations with other married men had been simply fly-by-night flings, often lasting no more than fifteen minutes. So if a married man spends only fifteen minutes, now and then, being unfaithful to his wife with only that one part of his body, he can claim that certainly for the most part he has been faithful.

I have known a number of married men who proclaimed these episodes of release as being, "Oh, it's nothing." Some of them were really something! And usually I did not care if they did not think anymore about it than shaking off the last drops of pee from the penis after taking a long and glorious leak. I got what I wanted – so, so long and good-bye.

It could not be that way with Terry Lane. Terry was not, could not be, a one-night stand.

Terry came into my heart as surely as the cream of his body came into my mouth and deep between my buttocks. Terry came.

The hours after, the day after, the nights after, Terry's body was not there, but the spirit of Terry was with me. There was an aura of Terry encircling my entire being. I lived and breathed in the atmosphere of Terry. He had made himself a part of me and I believe deep in my heart that he had made a part of himself.

A part. Not the whole. Not the entirety of oneself. Even without his wife and children there would be other parts of his life to which he had to give himself. His work, for instance. I had forgotten to ask him what type of work he did. It did not matter. He could be one of the leisurely rich or he could be a dishwasher, what did I care? Did I remember to tell him that I am a writer? Would he care? Could his children mean more to him than my books mean to me? I think that is one of the ways I solved the problem of his marriage. No, let me correct myself. I did not solve the problem. One of the ways I dealt with the fact was the realization that I was married, in a sense, to my creative spirit, and I have often thought of my books as my children.

I told myself: if he can deal with an author, I can deal with a married man.

I refused to let myself think much about his wife and children. I wandered around in a daze. My mind was inebriated with unworded thoughts of him, except for his words of love. We had fallen so quickly, so beautifully, so profoundly. This daze was his image – his nudity, the green of his eyes, those emeralds of mirrored bliss, his tongue, his lips, his mouth, his body, his buttocks, and the deep tightness between those exquisitely moulded buns.

I wanted to save my cream for him, save it until our date the following Sunday afternoon. But I could not. My hand went to my staff of divine life as images of him set upon my mind and body so clearly that I could not resist the palm and the staff and the images making love in a hazy-dream, and flying cream lighting upon my pillow behind my ear, the ear hearing the heart of reflection: 'I love you, Phillip. You love me too. I know you do. I feel your love for me."

My chest expanded in the aftermath of breathing, trying to breathe him back with me, trying to breathe him into me.

I could not think of it as a mere act of masturbation. It was far more than that, it was making love to the man who was not there in the flesh, but who was so much there in my heart that my flesh, caressing my flesh, became the solidity of his image. He was with me in all respects except the reality of the flesh.

Images of love, images of a lover, have been such a profound part of my life that I cannot skim over their importance to the mind. Sometimes I think I would have lost my mind, if I had not had the emotional reflection of a lover with me to comfort me in the aloneness of myself. For there in my palm I placed his lips with saliva and I let the imagined lips travel up and down the bigness of me, and he came so intensely into my mind he was all but there. He embraced me with invisible arms; yet my mind could see his arms encircling me; his hands of the mind, caressing me, touching me in reflective-imagined recreation of his true presence in the presence of a masturbatorial dream. I prolong his palmed-lips by momentarily interrupting the act long enough to change my middle finger into his remembered penis, and inserting the penis-finger into my anus and in the memory-mirror of my mind he makes anal love to me again, not so deep in reality as the reality of his rod had given me; yet he was dreamfully there and he sank, I believe, even deeper into my heart.

For there are men who only skate over the heart, but this man, my most beautiful lover, infiltrated me so engrossingly that he dug a passageway through all four chambers of my heart. And so the throbbing of my staff of life intensified so commandingly I had to withdraw my phallic-finger and give the palmed-lips of reflective-Terry to my staff again, and I sank into such a haze of him in my mind that I did not know the pounding of my heart from the remembered pounding of his heart; I did not know the throbbing of my staff of life from the throbbing of his rod of dreams.

God endowed me with this profound imagination.

So I possessed him again.

There was disappointment when my cream flew through the air, and he flew away from me, but I caught him again and brought him back to me in the dream that stirred in my heart.

His wife might know his physical presence, but I knew his dream-presence, and I comforted myself with this dream, and I came to believe his spirit was with me all through the day and all through the night.

I would kiss my pillow and my pillow became his cheeks, and I would sleep. And I would wait.

Chapter 6

DINNER WITH WALTER and Vera Smothers the following Friday evening remains, in some respects, vague. But I do remember clearly the changing of expressions in Walter's dark eyes. In certain light, at certain angles, Walter's eyes were as black as a starless night without a moon; in other lights, at other angles, they were as dark brown as the earth from the grave in which he buried so many desires. Desires that squirmed in the grave of himself, turned and twisted in the night, and stuck swords of gleaming, blinding flesh into his soul, and certainly influenced his obsession with literature as a knightly and honourable shield against those hidden and fascinating desires.

From the darkness of his eyes and, at times, from the tone of his voice, I saw and heard jealousy. Yet, I am sure, Vera simply interpreted her revered husband as being concerned about my welfare, worried because I had fallen in love with a married man.

And there was that true element in Walter's feelings, but she loved him with an old fashioned blind trust, therefore how could he possibly have any desires for me. I was simply his best friend, that is all. And since his best friend just happened to be a homosexual, that simply proved that Walter was an open-minded modern, not a hick from the South as he had been raised to be. They prided themselves in outgrowing their past, and I respected them for this, for they were in so many ways wondferful friends.

But that evening Walter's jealousy ceased to be amusing and became annoying. He made such remarks as, "You're too intelligent to fall for some guy who can't even give you half of himself. He not only has a wife, he has two kids."

"Yes, Walter. I know, Walter. But intelligence or lack of intelligence has nothing to do with love."

"Then what about your self respect? You are not just half a person to be treated as a part time lover. Aren't you a complete entity?"

"No man is a complete entity," I professed. "We are all simply parts and pieces of life, trying to get it together, trying to see, trying to know, where and how the parts and pieces fit into our everyday routine existence."

"Yes, yes," he said, glaring at me over a bite of mint jelly, glaring as if he resented me for having said something that he wished he had expressed in the clarity of the spoken word, for I know that Walter had these feelings of parts and pieces of the self even more than I. "I won't argue with you about that. But you don't have to let anyone treat you like you were just a piece of his life."

"I think he'll treat me like I am a part of his life."

"Walter," Vera urged hesitantly, "we have to realize it is Phillip's life. We can't run his life for him."

"I'm not trying to run his life. I'm just trying to enlighten him to the facts of life, the facts of reality."

"Oh, well," Vera said, cutting into another lamb chop. "They do say love is blind."

"Mine's not," Walter expostulated, and it is a good thing that poor lamb chop was dead, else it would have bleated to high heaven. "My eyes were wide open when I fell in love with you. Weren't your eyes open when you fell in love with me? Of course they were."

He did not give her a chance to say: *I have to close my eyes to some things.*

I could almost feel my flesh crawling with bits of his inhibition and bits of his jealousy. I think he felt most comfortable with me when I was being promiscuous. Matters of the flesh as only flesh tickled his own repressed desires, but when my heart became involved I think he felt more toward the surface of his feelings than he wanted to feel, an under the skin irritation, pinpricks of desire.

He would have liked to be the Walter that he presented to himself and his wife and to others, but he would also like to be another Walter, another self, one that could let go of all restraints, unzip the zipper on his mind, and pour himself into the arms of another man, and calm those bubbles that formed at the corners of his mouth.

But if he should ever release the prohibited Walter, the Walter he dimly sensed, the Walter who flowed in his blood and sometimes tossed and turned in his blood, if this Walter came out of his darkness he would quite possibly destroy the regular Walter; he could club him to death with phallic thrills and choke him with streams of wakened dreams.

The Walter who sat at the table that evening could deal with himself reasonably well so long as his lie about the existence of the other Walter persisted. He acknowledged that no one was one hundred per cent heterosexual nor was there anyone who was one hundred per cent homosexual. This was the modern way of thinking open-mindedly. He thought his degree of homosexuality was merely an intellectual recognition. He did not know he hungered for it; he did not know he looked upon me as a tender morsel to be devoured if ever he cut loose with those beaten down appetites.

He was distantly gnawing upon me at the dinner table. I was more amused than irritated. He had a second serving of lamb chops.

However, I suppose Walter was the only one who was fully there that evening. Vera was sitting on the sidelines – Vera usually sat on the sidelines of Walter. I was there physically, but I was out somewhere floating on an emotional cloud of romantic dreams. Terry Lane came between myself and anything or anyone else. He was a veil of flesh, a curtain of flesh, a dream of flesh.

His beauty stood between me and whatever Walter was saying.

Walter and Vera hardly existed. So far as I was concerned they did not need to exist. I was making this visit as a routine matter of life, a matter that didn't matter. Generally their friendship meant a lot to me. They were part of that heterosexual society that accepted me, and no one respected my creativity more than Walter. They were both extremely well read and we could spend hours discussing literature.

But I had fallen so deeply and so beautifully in love that

nothing else mattered to me except Terry. Terry, in his absence, was there for me more than Walter and Vera.

Terry did not hear Walter say: "Emotional danger is just as serious as physical danger."

And I only vaguely heard myself say: "Yes, Walter. I know, Walter."

In my mind I knew he was talking about me. Emotionally I felt he was out on a limb in some distant forest, talking to somebody else, talking about somebody I had not even met. Not me. Not myself. Not my love. Walter was far gone. Vera was picking violets under the shadow of Walter's tree.

There was lemon chiffon pie for dessert. The chiffon had always made me think of cum. Dreamfully, I ate a big slice.

Walter was saying, "Always wondered how the chiffon of this kind of pie stays up. Looks like it is going to collapse and fall flat, but it never does."

I let it slide down my throat.

I looked completely through Walter and I saw Terry. I looked at Vera, an expert cook, telling how chiffon held up, and she wasn't there. Terry was there, stark naked, his belly covered with chiffon.

It always had been my favourite pie.

"More coffee?" Vera asked.

"Yes, thank you."

She poured. "Walter, pass Phillip the cream."

Oh, God, yes. I bit my lip to hold back the words. Yes, but not from Walter. Let Terry give it to me.

Everything was in a spermatic whirl.

I swallowed my dreams.

Chapter 7

I OPENED MY eyes Sunday morning and knew this was the day I would see Terry again. I felt the confidence of knowing he would keep his word, the beauty of trust.

Dear God, hell and damnation, how many times with how many men had we made dates and one or the other failed to show up? I give myself credit for generally keeping my word. But so many times I would be sitting on a bar stool waiting for Tom, Dick or Harry, Bill, Jack or Joe, and I would be waiting for promises that someone had forgotten, maybe even deliberately broken, promises made simply for the sake of sounding warm at the time of the making, or promises made in all sincerity but later reconsidered and shoved aside. For a million reasons or no reason. Flippancy always annoyed me. Yet, between love affairs, I never turned down a handsome quickie.

(Where have all the lips gone, lips that wandered into my life, lived and lied and disappeared? How many beautiful lips, lips entranced in ecstasy – vanished lips! Starving. Hungry. Floating from pillar to post. (Oh, ye beloved Freudian symbols, stand up and proclaim yourselves.) Butterfly lips lighting on stalks of bright red flowers. Flitting, flitting … Flitting away. But not just other lips. My lips too. How many red flowers have my lips known? How many stalks have stalked away and hidden themselves in the fly of good bye?)

"Hello," he said; the word, just that one word trembled his lips when I opened the door and lights of emerald green glittered in his eyes.

"Hello," mine was a whisper, clogging halfway up my throat. My eyes felt watery.

For a moment we simply stood there. Terry, just outside the doorway. Myself, just inside the doorway. The gaze, our mutual gaze, had to be devoured. Our eyes drew in the presence of one another. We saw, we believed, and we believed in the unbelievable beauty of our second meeting. He was here. His eyes were kissing my eyes with the intensity of the gaze. He was here. He was not like so many others. I knew he would be here. I had to believe. He was not like the fly-by-night contents of the fly of so many others. He was here.

"May I come in?" His words trembled with the trembling of his lips.

"Please," I said, and the drawing in of my breath seemed to draw him into my foyer, and he was in my arms. I don't remember the door closing, but it must have closed. Of course, it closed. It could not stay open. I don't remember locking the door. Maybe I didn't.

I remember being in his arms. His arms around my waist; my arms around his waist; our lips so united as to become the flesh of each other; our saliva bathing the tongue of each other; our hands rushing from the waist to the shoulders to draw us closer than close; our hands wandering, caressing, finding the buttocks, between the buttocks; our hearts beating out the rhythm of ecstasy; our minds dazed, unthinking, swirling; our genitals growing, pressing his against mine, pressing mine against his – phallic mirrors.

He whispered something into my mouth.

"What?" I asked. I thought I heard what he said, but I had to make sure.

"I love you," a whispering of the lips and the mouth and the tongue, and oh God, yes, the heart had to be there too, our whispering hearts, speaking into the mouth, speaking into my heart, mine speaking into his – surely, surely, just as if God had created the heart to speak as distinctly as the vocal chords, and with far more depths of honesty.

"I love you," saying this, the nature of myself gave him what he was giving me.

Our souls embraced.

We were an aura of ourselves.

The invisibility of our souls became almost visible in the

intensity of our love.

We could not break the embrace. We did not try. We breathed into each other. We became the breath of one another. His tongue was doing something to my neck, my throat, my chest. He sank to his knees, and loosened my fly, and said, "I worship you." And the God up above, the one God, the true God, was not jealous or offended. He understood the Heaven of our creation, and He was pleased with the joy that issued forth from those of His creation. He blessed us in the silence of bliss. He gave us ourselves.

We are the rapture of his creation; we are the fruition of this our Garden of Eden.

We surpass the ordinary.

We are beyond the humdrum.

We are the earth of ourselves; we are gay laughter; we are inverted loneliness; we are a queer juxtaposition of joy and sorrow, we drink celestial juices of one another; the pineapples and the oranges bow to us; we squeeze the lemons, and we have known as many lemons as we have known stars; we are so terribly human, so beautfiully human.

"Terry. Terry. Stand up to me. Wait."

I drew him up to me, my body wanting the explosion of myself before I was ready to give vent to the stars of my mind, and I leaned over slightly – he was perhaps three-quarters of an inch shorter than myself – and I gave my tongue to his hunger, clenching my buttocks, holding back the fluidity of the stars in my loins, drawing my crotch slightly away from the fires of him, lest I lose my cream before the time of its giving.

He who knows all, did He at the time of our creation know we were destined to meet and take armfuls of heaven unto ourselves and cause the very same heavens to quake in our arms?

Isn't it more reasonable to think that we were created for love, rather than for wars and hate and slurs and all those negative things of the ordinary common world?

Love is the reason for being.

We are our reason for being. The rod and the staff of gay lovers pressing together, silently shouted for the nakedness of each other. We were stiff with longing. It was hard for us to separate long enough to undress. But somehow, arms releasing, arms embracing, we managed to undress each other. He was on his knees again, removing my shoes and licking my balls. So it was only fair that I should kneel to him and remove his shoes, and I savoured the hanging balls of him. Jewels of flesh I have never understood the workings of, but ah how silently and beautifully they work for us!

I tasted the moisture on the shining rod of him.

"Oh, my God!" he exclaimed. "There has never been anyone like you." And I knew he was telling me that this was better than being with his wife. I went all the way down, transposing paradise into the flesh even as the flesh became paradise; he withdrew, as he leaned over, his buttocks going eight or nine inches away from me; he grasped me under my arms and lifting me up to his lips, as he said, "Wait. The bed the bed the bed."

We left everything there in the foyer, except our socks which we had forgotten to take off. We kissed our way into the bedroom and onto the bed. (I had already removed the spread while waiting for him.) Our hands roamed through fields of lean flesh, discovering and rediscovering the touch of each other. Touching me, his hands turned on lights in my eyes and the lights were made of diamonds, and I felt as if my eyes themselves were having an orgasm at this touch with his beauty. His hard chest was covered with soft flesh and the beating of his heart drew my mouth to the tit over his heart, and I sucked upon the beating of his heart.

I was over him, my left hand slightly under his right shoulder, and while my lips were tasting the drums of heaven-in-his-ribs, my right hand wandered around and found the deep crevice between his buttocks, and I played with the golden hairs around his hole of penetrating dreams.

I heard his sighs and I was blessed with his sighs, and I heard my name uttered through his sighs, and the sounds of him came to me as a voice from his blood, yearning and calling to me. And so I sank down and I filled my heart and my soul with the staff of him, a staff as wise in its way as the staff of the wise men in the olden days we read about in the Scriptures, for the wisdom of the flesh finds its soul in the arms of love, and there is no profane love – all love is sacred.

And so it was I worked with the wisdom of the flesh in the mouth of my soul until he gave me the juices of heaven, and I swallowed a part of heaven even as I swallowed a part of the man. Then I held quietly upon the limbering staff as I knew he would have me do, for his hands held my head down while his fingers played in the hairs of my head as though he were counting them, entering them in a thousand dreams of times like this, my bowed head upon his loins.

Heaven need not forgive us, for heaven can only praise us, for only heaven, united with the intimate abilities of man, can give us such supreme paradise.

I simply wanted to rest in the serenity of this aftermath. So quietly my fingers played again with the soft golden hairs around the hole of tightness, knowing when I wished, the lock of his buttocks would be unlocked. But now my left cheek rested on a mound of blond pubic-haired gold, and I was rich with him in the powerful value of love.

Our silence lingered in this golden dream of wakefulness, and we inhaled the aroma of his orgasm; I could feel, at the time of his coming, the tingling fibres in his legs, and now I felt as if I had drunk not only the cream of him but even the tingling fibres of him. I savoured these matters of his flesh, in dreams and reality, and I did not know the dreams from the reality. His body became a poem of interpenetrated touches.

The poem was delicious to my soul.

His soul made a journey into my heart, and I heard him whisper my name, "Phillip," and his voice spoke in the softness of our souls.

"Terry." I returned the whisper with his name, tasting his name on my lips.

"Phillip... Phillip ... Come to me." His thighs began to open. "Come inside me. Make the inside of me yours."

He opened his legs and lifted them up, and I sank my face there between the pillars of an angel, and I pressured his hips upward until my lips found and set upon the entrance of him, and I moistened with soul-kisses this beloved entrance; then I lifted my body over and above him and my belly touched his belly of milk-white dreams, and my lips grabbed in greedy hunger the food of his lips, while my key of flesh pressed and unlocked the gates of anal paradise, and the trembling of his buttocks played within my blood as I gave the intimacy of myself to him, and I was an angel of manliness piercing the halo of the backside of a heavenly man.

He was so far beyond the ordinary, that is why I cannot think of that divine crevice as being what is commonly called an asshole. When people are peeved with people; when people are angry with others, they refer to them as an asshole. They do not speak in praise of the ass, nor do they speak in praise of the hole. They speak derogatively. No! Not I. Not with reference to Terry Lane. He transposed the ordinary to a golden halo of flesh deep between his buttocks. My staff was in heaven.

Shepherds, guiding their sheep, pause in the meadows and touch upon their staffs and silently pray for the good of man.

In me, in Terry, their prayers are answered.

Did they, the wandering Shepherds, did they wander upon one another and find within one another the internal meadows of celestial bliss? Did one become an angel within the other; did the other become an angel for the one within?

Were the wise men wise enough to find the shining red rubies upon themselves? Did they kneel in reverence and drink the liquid silver of male paradise?

We are many and we have been many; the years have known us, even as I knew Terry there in my arms that late afternoon, even before the sun had set on the Lord's day. Our world was not a new world – it was simply born again with each new impregnation of love, for we gave birth to one another's love; we gave birth to the art of love.

I rode on and within the halo of him until the riding created a tingling in my very toes and ankles, and the tingling travelled up into and through my calves, and into my thighs, and there came from within me an explosion of liquid stars that caused me to bite into his neck, and his fingers left marks upon my back as they roamed the route of ecstasy.

How could this time be even better than the other? I do not know. God is my witness, I know it to be true – time becomes a betterment of itself in the deepening of the lover's love.

I rested between the pillars of paradise while his toes

caressed my buttocks. I felt the beating of our hearts, beating against one another. I felt a serenade in our silence, and he sang songs of love to me in my blood, unheard by the ear of hearing, only felt in the clarity of the blood-song.

We were entranced.

Love came to us and touched us.

And passion was its manifestation; passion was its revelation. The mirrored loins of gay love thus joined in the joys of love.

We were at rest for perhaps ten or fifteen minutes, with only whispers, now and then of one another's name, and words of love: "My love"... "I love you"... "Love"... The simplicity was as lovely as complicated lace.

I was all along aware of his semi-erection pressing against my belly, the fullness of it had given way to the fullness of my own while I was within him; now I could feel it growing in its intensity, and my belly yearned to open for him but it could not. And I wondered which way he would prefer, and I asked him with whispers in his ear: "Do you want me this way, the way I have you? Or do you want me to turn over? Or do you want me to go down on you?"

There was a pause, and then in slight laughter, he answered, "All those ways. All the ways we can think of."

I gave him whispered laughter in return and said, "We will. But which way first?"

He kissed my lips and tongued my tongue. "This way," and he gave his tongue to my mouth.

Slowly, I withdrew my staff from the halo of him, and I saw that I was clean and he was clean, so I let myself slide down to his golden halo of golden hairs and I kissed the hole of dreams in the reality of ourselves. And thus I entered into a golden daze of ecstasy as I tasted upon his delights, and I took first one ball of paradise into my mouth and then the other and I took care not to squeeze the balls of paradise too hard, and then slowly his legs, those pillars of Heaven, fell down so I went down all the way from the crowned ruby of him to the root of his desire, and back again and again, and oh my God my God, the depths and the heights of it was a ladder of bliss upon which my lips played and my tongue worked, and I was a carpenter building a house of dreams wherein there would be living stars for him to know in the coming of their fleeting presence. And as the stars came to him, from him, through him, out of him, I felt the coming of his stars and I felt and saw the flashes in my own eyes, and I drank the stars he had so miraculously changed into liquid.

Thus I say unto you, my beloved gay readers, the staff of a gay man is no less miraculous than the staff of Moses who brought and gave miracles to his people, and we, even we ourselves, may and do bring miracles to one another (and now I flash into the present, from then into the now of ourselves, and say, though there be sorrow amongst us in this day of plague, we shall through the miracle of love and God overcome and surpass these sad sorrows).

Life in itself is a miracle; that we love is a miracle among the origin of miracles, for love may thus, in being itself, surpass the crimes of the day and the crimes of the night, shield itself, protect the hearts of our loves from the outrageous and the petty meanness of common, ordinary day by day stresses upon the lives of us as we walk and work and sometimes merely exist in the trials of living.

Thus it is to cherish the miracles of ourselves as we embrace our loves and draw the curtain between the time of lovers and the time of plodding and the time of death.

Oh, how tenderly he gave me the power of himself!

What raptures my love and I shared.

I drank till he was empty.

And I was filled with delight.

Oh, my love, how the youth of our years treated us with repeated voyages into one another!

We were so magnificient the memory weighs upon me and tires me, so I must lay down my pen and rest a while for I am exhausted.

...My memory goes back to him; he comes back to me; it is just as though we were young again, feeling the vibrations of youth. How lovingly youth longs for one another, how tremendous the hungers of youth! The mouth of the heart is wide for love, craving one more taste of the beloved. Times of rest are unsought and resented. We did not want to relax between our journeys to paradise. And there were times when we did not pause, and on that night, the second time of our times together, that was a time of no respite. I had not swallowed down all the stars when I felt him drawing me up to him as he was sliding down to me, to my lips, and his mouth reached for my mouth and he tasted the stars of himself, stars still floating in my saliva. And I could feel the bliss of his hunger; I could feel the ecstasy of his thirst.

"It's almost like drinking myself," he whispered. "You saved some of it for me, didn't you?" And I whispered into the moisture of his lips: "I could feel you wanting it." And we exchanged saliva with each other, and we trembled in the exchange. "Take me again," he said. "Again the same way. Then let me help you drink it." And so I slid down to him again, and he was still erect and full in his desire, and the jewel and the root of himself were mine again – ah, the ruby of his head, the gold of his root – we were rich in our desires, rich with our love, and overflowing with the fluidity of silver stars. So it was this time I did not swallow the stars, my mouth overflowing with the celestial juices of him, I quickly gave him my lips and he took himself into himself and caressed his very own tongue with the internal release of himself, and then with loving care returned the liquid stars to me, and around inside my mouth I again tasted the liquid of his internal self and returned to him what had not slipped down all the way into the depths of me, and he took it in good delight and let it slowly flow down into him, and it was as if he had swallowed himself even as I had swallowed him, and in the swallowing of the maleness, we swallowed the stars, and heaven was our gift to one another.

We were the answer to Adam's loneliness. Eve betrayed him. We were the answer. The eternal answer. We shall flow and ever flow, and flow forever.

Even as I am now floating upon the juices of memory and the memory of juices, I feel again his tender caresses in the afterglow. I see him again on these pages as though they were not pages but the living flesh of him. I hold my pen as though it were not a pen – I hold it as though it were his penis. For he is and forever more shall be the *is* of time, not the *was* of time. I merely add the word *is* to the word *pen*, and

I have penis, and it is his and it is mine.

We never parted. We could not have parted. It was only the mistake of time that caused us to think we had parted. We became such a part of each other, we were together even though apart. In the time upon time, the time after time, we saw each other, we lined ourselves internally with the fluidity of the inner depths of each other, and it was as if our souls melted and did flow one into the other, and it was not so much an exchange of souls as it was an intermingling, an interlacing of our souls till we were internally one, even though our external selves were two. But the two of us felt the other, although we were apart far more than we were together in the flesh of ourselves. He felt my soul walking with him wherever he stepped, from step to step, day by day, night after night. I know it is so for he told me so. And I breathed his soul with my breath and my soul, and we were truly as one soul with two bodies.

Thus it was that Manhattan disappeared. The buildings, the concrete, the world of business, the garbage, the people, the roaring noise. All disappeared, and we were in a Garden of Eden, the Garden of Gay Delights. Our love had melted away all external things, and they were merely an illusion to be ignored, even in dealing with them, until we were together again.

Yet our Garden came to life only once a week. Late Sunday afternoon till midnight. This was his time of freedom, his time, as he said, "to become the real me".

"I am not myself when we are not together. This is another person, someone who has stolen my body away from me and goes around living under my name, just as if he was really myself. But he knows he isn't. He only pretends. That person loves my wife and my son. He is actually the father of my sons. Sometimes it is hard for me to believe. And I love my wife and sons, Phillip. I can't fool you. But I am someone else, another person, the other me, is false even in his goodness. Sometimes I don't really know him. Simply because he is living in my skin doesn't mean I really know him. He is a stranger walking around inside myself, dealing with his wife, my wife, caring for his sons who are my sons.

He works as a stranger to myself. And the stranger comes to know himself, myself, only when I walk out of my house in Brooklyn and start toward you. The closer I come to you, Phillip, the more acquainted I become with myself. And when we are together, then it is, then is when I know and feel who I am. The real me. The real person. I can throw away all pretenses. I can try, but only try to forget that other person. And oh my God, Phillip, when we are making love, I actually do, honest to God, I forget that other guy. There is no one but you. I don't have a wife. I don't have children. That huge pretentious world does not exist. Everything and everyone fades away in your arms. You love them out of me. You suck me into the real world of myself."

We lived for those times when we would be together, all else was merely existing. I was writing a book length prose poem, so I was able to sublimate the frustrations of our times apart – I gave to the poem what I could not give to him.

In his way, he gave to his wife and sons what he could not give to me. But I could not think about that part of his life, I could not let it linger in my mind. I do not believe I was jealous, but I might have been, if I had let my thoughts drift in that direction. I closed my mind to his family life. Through a drawn shade I could dimly see the shadows of that other life. I did not want to lift the shade. I did not want to open the door to something that would have brought sorrow into my mind and turn my heart into a bitter kernel.

Yet that may have happened if I were not a writer. I gave so much love to the creation of a manuscript, how could I blame him for giving love to his wife and sons. There were times when I wondered if he still loved his wife with a romantic love. When he referred to his love for her, it sounded more like duty than love, a duty he had to perform for the mother of his children. I knew he loved his sons. (If only my father had loved me nearly as much as Terry loved his sons, my childhood would have been less frightened.) He was concerned about what they would think if they ever found out their father had another life with someone other than their mother.

"I wish they could know, and love me and respect me, in

knowing all about me, as much as they do in knowing only a part."

I did not ask him questions about his family. As time went along I perceived that it was best for him to release anything he needed to release, and only when his mood was ripe for releasing. I had, at one point, made a slight mistake in questioning him about his wife, and the expression on his face, in his eyes, seemed to fall. He answered the question, he answered politely. But his attitude was one of prickly pain. I had opened a door that only he could open without it disturbing him.

I believe he sorrowed more than I about his inability to spend more time with me. "It's my fault, all my fault, my God, how I want you every day and every night."

"I want you too, believe me I do. But we have these Sunday evenings. And you never leave my heart. When you walk out that door, you leave a part of you with me. A part I love seven times more than anyone else could possibly love."

I wish I had known how to tell him not to blame himself for anything. I wish I had known how to tell him not to put himself down or feel any fault within himself for being away from me.

I was at a time of my youth when I did not know how to help him free himself from any seed of negativity that might, in the years to come, cause or influence the cause of any serious disturbance.

I was seeped in the beauty of my creative spirit, writing that long poem, and a very difficult play followed the poem. So perhaps there was something about me that would not have known how to handle a full time lover. Somehow the time of our Sundays together spilled over into the other six days and six nights of the week. There were times when I truly felt the spirit of him, the spirit of his love, his spirit was holding me close to him even while we were apart.

When I told him about this feeling he said a little pensively, "I think about you all the time, even when maybe I shouldn't be thinking about you, but I do. I no longer reach for my wife in bed. When she reaches for me, I perform the act, but I am thinking about you even then. I believe she knows I am not really there, but she doesn't say anything. Sometimes I feel her straining too hard to please me. I spend more time with her, Phillip, but I share more time with you in actually making love. There is a difference in spending time and in sharing time. I hope I am not being cruel to her. I try not to be. She knew I was bisexual when I asked her to marry me, and I never promised her I would give it up. She realizes this is a part of my life I must have. I have to have it. I have to have you, Phillip. The more I love you, the less I feel of my heterosexual life, the more I feel deep in my gay life. I cannot regret the other side of me, no matter which side I am looking at. It's only that I wish I could be with you all the time, and I know I can't."

Even though there were others in his life who were close to him, very close, I believe he felt more lonely when we were not together than I felt. Each time we met he held me as though he had been craving for me all his life, not just for a week, but a lifetime of craving came into his love-making. He gave me seven times more of the intensity of love than any other man had given me. And I loved him seven times more than I had ever loved any other man.

I was the part of his life that was away from the ordinary, the commonly accepted way of life. And Terry Lane was far from being ordinary, far from being common. In appearance he might have been a model, in vibrancy he might have been an actor. In his work he was a dynamic young advertising executive. In my arms, he was mine.

He let me know I was the true side of himself. Not that these other sides were false, it is simply that his life with me was, he believed, the real life he was born to live.

There were times when the emeralds of his eyes teared with undropped tears at parting. His lips would tremble. His body clothed, now at the door, would quiver in my arms. "Help me to leave. I have to go. Don't let me weaken. Give me strength." And I would, with him still in my arms, walk him out the door, draw his arms from around me, kiss the fingers of his hands, and say, "I love you." Then quickly I let myself inside my apartment and closed the door upon the flesh of my dreams, as I went on dreaming.

Chapter 8

MY DAYS, MY nights... without him...

I suppose I, too, became something of another person. Just as important to my life as any man's wife and children were the writing of books and plays. In this way, to some degree, I understood Walter's theory that literature was more important than life, or that life was meaningless without the arts. However, if I had been born without a creative spirit, if six days and six nights of my life were a blank, life would have been worth living for just that one evening a week with my beloved Terry. But I could not or would not place his wife and children above my books, plays, and poems. I seem to recall reading somewhere that such diverse writers as Thomas Mann and Pearl Buck gave precedence to their creativity over their children. That is the power and the force of the creative spirit. Family oriented people may think this shocking or foolish or insulting to the family life of all "decent minded" people. Tough shit. I have always felt that what we do with our brain cells is just as important as what we do with our sperm cells.

Sometimes I tried to talk to Terry about my creative spirit; he listened respectfully and with admiration, but I know he did not understand the depth of its meaning for me. Did I fully understand the importance of Terry's family to him? I don't know. I simply accepted. I never attempted to take him away from his wife. That would have been cutting him in half. That would have destroyed a part of him. I do not believe I could have taken him away from his family even if I had tried. I know no one could possibly cause me to give up writing.

I think equating his family with my books helped me to

adjust to this love I bore for that beautiful married man, the man who occasionally shared his body with a woman but slept with her overnight. I had enough imagination to write books, but my imagination never went far enough to see an image of him making love to her. Actually I believe he stopped making love to her even before we began our affair. He simply dipped his thing into a duty-bound vessel, moved it a while, and took it out again. "That thing" which became to me and for me a divine staff of love.

There are times when the mind goes where the heart goes.

And yet he came to me everyday and every night. The presence of a lover's spirit in a heart can be as strong as the body. It is simply not as tangible. You cannot wrap your arms around the image of a man, but the spirit of that man can come inside you and wrap itself around your heart. When the two of you become united as one you can feel his heart beating in rhythm with your heart even though he may be talking with his wife and sons in a house in Brooklyn while you are writing a poem in an apartment in Manhattan. There are those who would say this is imagination, "you're dreaming it up", and even though I respect my imagination and love my dreams, I believe belief is more than that – I believe it is the spirit of love, I believe it is the union of two lovers united in such close intimacy that they are never truly apart, no matter where the bodies roam, no matter where the bodies have to go or have to stay. The intangibility of the spirit frequently causes denial of the spirit and even with those who believe in it, we often forget or do not feel the power of this intangibility. The spirit can give the heart the comfort it needs, the spirit can soothe the body. The body and the heart can drive the mind insane if the spirit fails.

The spirit of our love was a God-send.

The spirit of my love moved in the palm of my hand with my saliva and he was in the heart of me when my flesh lifted up and cried out in the silent roar of my blood for his sensual presence.

I told him of these times and he said to me, "I am glad you feel my presence even when I am not with you. I am with you even when your eyes do not see me because I know our love is deeper than our eyes. I think I can feel you masturbating with my spirit in your palm. You may not understand, no, I know you will understand, even though my wife is there and ready for me at anytime, I turn to her only when she reaches for me. But last week when she reached for me, I turned away and said I was too tired. That day in the office you were so much on my mind, I could not think clearly about my work. I had to go into the men's room, close myself off in a stall, drop my pants, sit back on the stool and feel you with me. My saliva became your mouth. The power of your love, the power of your spirit, had lifted my cock so intensely that I felt vibrations in my hand, and I caught in my handkerchief what I wanted to give to you. Phillip, our love is growing deeper. Our love is growing more intense. It's been almost three years now and our love is even more beautiful now than it was in the beginning. So often the initial intensity of a gay romance is just a prelude to the end. Ours must never end, Phillip. Never. Oh my God, Phillip, I don't belong to my office, I don't belong to my wife, I don't belong to my sons, I belong to you, Phillip, I give them my time, I give them my duty, that means I am simply out on loan to them. I am always giving you my heart. You drift around in my mind like a breeze in a field of flowers. I take out my prick to take a leak, and I do not see my hand there holding it – it's your hand, and you shake the last drops off for me. You enter my loins and heart and blood and you are with me more than all my surroundings. I am the only one who sees you, I am the only one who feels you, but I know you are with me. I have to feel your mouth in the palm of my hand. I cannot masturbate at night with my wife there beside me, although I want you so much sometimes it hurts, so I have to do it in the men's room at the agency where I work. I know you are with me, wherever you go, whatever I do. Your heart beats in my heart. You are becoming more and more my world, Phillip, and everything, everyone else is simply hanging on outside my real world, wrapped around me, tied to me, duty bound to me, duty duty duty. My God, I hate my duty. Yet I respect myself for performing my duty. Sometimes I hate my duty, even though I love those I perform it for."

"Do not hate it too much," I warned.

I was afraid his hate for his duty might infiltrate his love for his family and become a mixture of love and hate, a duel within himself of love and hate. I did not really believe his love for me could be killed in the duel, but I feared it. He gave me so much love, it was hard for me to believe he was capable of hating anything or anyone. But he was human, very human, so very very human.

I rarely thought of him as being a mere man – there was something god-like about him, man as god or god as man, but when he spoke of hatred for his duty, I realized he was only mortal. I never wanted him to step down from the pedestal I had put him upon.

And strangely (or is it understandable?) he was never higher on that pedestal than while he was kneeling to me.

It was hard for me to imagine him on his job, performing his duty. Perhaps if we had lived together, seeing him and being with him in the flesh every day, I would have been able to understand more clearly his conflict between hating his duty and respecting himself for performing his duty. When he was with me, it was only on rare occasions that he revealed there was a conflict going on inside himself.

We were so intense in our passions that we did not want to discuss any of life's negativities.

We lived in a pink cloud of romance for eleven years, and it was a beautiful pink cloud, and it was a beautiful romance. We wanted only the beauty of love, the beauty of each other, the beauty of our nudity.

We did not think of the end of it all, nor the end of any part of it; we did not think about the end of anything. Each meeting was a new beginning for a new time of ecstasy. We were lovers-supreme. Our Sundays were our lives, the true times of our lives. The other six days and six nights were fringes on a pivot of life. We lived for one day a week, and not even a full day. He usually arrived at three in the afternoon and left at midnight.

We did not go to the theatre, the movies, or to the bars. Occasionally we took a stroll in Central Park.

We did not want the outside world to infringe upon our romance. If it was imperfect in its time limitations, it was as perfect as we could possibly make it in our times together.

And we let the beauty of our Sundays overflow from one week to the next, sustaining us in our love, lift us through whatever we needed to go through to get by from one day to the other, through those six days and six nights apart.

I did not realize, at the time, how much his life was split.

I did not blame myself then, nor do I blame myself now, for the splitting of his life. There was no blame, there was no fault. I do not accept for myself nor for him such derogatory labels as blame or fault. He was a bisexual man with two lives to live. He was as God created him to be.

And if one side of his life began to overpower the other side, that was due to the nature of love, the intensity, the power. What man, what human being, lives on an even keel everyday, every night, of his life? If one side becomes more than the other, can it be honestly accused of being an imbalance?

Let he who is without an imbalance in his life cast the first stone.

I knew Terry Lane as a well-balanced man.

I had heard and read about many bisexuals who looked upon themselves as having the best of both worlds.

The world is not always at its best. The world gets a little slippery at times.

We gave each other our best.

Things out yonder, the world out yonder, life outside my apartment, faded away into the unseen, while we were together. Who or whatever else existed disappeared on our Sundays.

We sank into the beauty of each other. We lifted ourselves to the celestial heights of romance and fed each other our liquid stars. We drew a veil between ourselves and the outside world, and if the veil was made of intangibles, then so is the spirit of love.

I was seldom, seldom, haunted by the ghost of his love for his wife. I knew the ghost existed. But I believed, I trusted, the ghost was left in Brooklyn.

As the months and the years went along, I sensed the fading of the source of the ghost, while the vapor of the ghost became more ominous, but I was not aware of any underlying danger.

I never met her. I never saw her, not until later, and that was under very different circumstances. He rarely referred to her.

Still, somewhere, hidden away, somewhere there existed my lover's wife.

I remember one time specifically holding his erection in my hand, gazing at the opening in the ruby of it, and I was amazed in my realization that from out of that there had sprung the seed that grew into his two sons. I felt a quick, slight, passing tinge of resentment. Then I wiped away the amazement and the resentment. I would not let such feelings shit upon our romance.

Our love was too beautiful for the disturbances of reality.

Those seed should mean no more to me than the seed he gave to his handkerchief while he sat upon the stool in a stall, closed away somewhere in the business world. Indeed, those seed in the handkerchief meant more to me – I knew they contained thoughts of me. The seed that became his son sprang from him years before he had met me. They meant nothing to me. Nothing.

I never asked to see a picture of his wife, nor of his sons.

They had more of his time. I had more of the depths of him. This I believed. This I knew. Thus I comforted myself.

His spirit walked with me. His spirit talked with me. His spirit came with me into the Garden of my Dreams and he made love to me in the palm of my hand, even while we were bodily apart. We realized the gay spirit of ourselves.

Let her ghost fade where it may.

The spirit overpowered the ghost.

Yet from out of the darkness of him, the unspoken darkness, I sometimes sensed a fearful warning.

I put it aside. I had to. I did not question him.

Occasionally I saw a tinge of worry in those beautiful emeralds. I did not stir up the tinge. I did not trouble the trouble. I tried to make it go away by loving him all the more. Sometimes I simply softly kissed each eyelid, and then he would open his eyes and look at me with untroubled warmth. I did not want to pry into his family life. I had to pretend they did not exist. I did not deny their existence. I knew I was pretending. But I never doubted that his love for me went deeper inside him than his love for his family. He was a duty-bound man, but not completely bound. Duty was more honoured at the time of our romance (during the mid-forties on into the mid-fifties) than it is today. Duty was like a badge upon a man's soul; duty was a decoration upon a man's uniform of life. He simply performed it and that was that. Generally there was not love in the duty, it was somewhere on the fringes of it. Love saw the duty and duty saw the love.

As the years of our romance went along, I could sense the lessening of the love in his duty toward his wife. What had been love became more of a habit associated, connected with duty. His love for his sons was a steady love even though there were times when he seemed amazed at being a father.

In the business world he advanced from an assistant executive to an associate executive, then to a full-fledged executive; he was promoted numbers of times, from a group head to a department head, from small accounts to large accounts. I was proud of him, although that part of his life held little interest for me. My interest was in his feelings about it.

He had the ability to leave any business problems in his office. He never shared them with me, and I doubt he ever shared them with his wife. He shared them with his business associates. I believe he knew how to nip such problems in the bud before they occurred. Once he said to me: "Business is business. My family is my family. You are my main love. You are the center of my life. More of my heart and soul belongs to you than to anyone or anything else. Please believe me, you are inside of me even when you are not inside me. Your heart comes more deeply inside me than your sex comes in my throat or my ass. It is you that is sleeping with me, even though it is the body of my wife there beside me."

And with no one beside me in the reality of life, my dreams and his spirit surpassed reality and his heart and his soul were there with me.

Being physically alone does not mean one is entirely alone.

We loved across time.

Our Sundays were connected by the depths of our love.

He believed in the spirit as much as I did.

He also felt, with faith in our feelings, that some elements of our semen became absorbed into the internal skin of ourselves, his into mine and mine into his, our cells absorbed something of each other's semen.

Medical science, biology and psychology might declare that absurd, but we did not. We were not of the sciences, we were of love.

Our bodies embraced so intimately that more than once he whispered, "I was born to love you. Our love is our destiny. You are my destiny. We are the essence of each other."

He was speaking my thoughts, as well as his own. He was translating our feelings into the whispered word. There were times when we were so close I could not tell the beating of my heart from the beating of his heart.

Yet we were together, in that domineering thing called reality, only nine hours a week.

We did not starve between times. We hungered. We drank our dreams, we fed upon our fantasies. I was faithful to him and I know there was no one else for him, except that occasional dark dip into his wife, by invitation only. I am sure that never once, since our first time together did he initiate relations with his wife. He indicated to me that such episodes were becoming less frequent and were mechanical.

"I suppose it isn't fair to her," he said on one of those rare evenings when he needed to talk about his family, "but I am what I am."

She had him, but I had the best of him.

"Where does Daddy go on Sunday afternoons? Where was he till late at night, Mama?"

Those were touchy questions for his wife to answer.

Worst of all had been the questions and implications from their neighbors:

"Your husband seems to go out somewhere every Sunday afternoon. I couldn't sleep well last night and, sitting on my front porch, I saw him come in long after midnight. You sure he's not cheating on you?"

No doubt the wife I didn't know, whose husband had been in my arms, wanted to spit in their faces, but she had found a somewhat stable answer: "He belongs to an Advertising Club that meets every Sunday afternoon and goes on till midnight."

"I wouldn't let my husband belong to such a club."

"They have to entertain the Clients. Sometimes Clients come into New York City from such far away places as Ohio, or Chicago or Indianapolis, and the Executives have to entertain them. Business diplomacy is terribly important in the Advertising business."

A part of what she said was true. Diplomacy, called asskissing (terribly different from the way Terry and I did it) was just as important as saccharine. Clients frequently came in from out of town to New York City, but any entertaining was usually done during business hours, such as taking the Client to lunch, or if it was after business hours, the Client was taken to dinner or to the theater. It was not always necessary for an Agency Executive to accompany the Clients to the theater, rarely would only one representative of a Client appear. And on such rare occasions one of the Executives would accompany the Client. And it was even more rare for a Client to stay the entire weekend. However, this had occurred once, and Terry had given this as an excuse to his wife to give to the inquisitive neighbors.

After a while the neighbors stopped asking questions and thought what they wanted to think.

For himself, Terry did not care what the neighbors thought. For his wife and children, he did care, but he said, "Some things I simply have to let her handle the best way she can."

She must have known his love for her had gradually diminished. Many married couples tell themselves this is bound to happen through the years. "Nobody's honeymoon lasts forever." And the weight of the years can take the blame for a lot of marital problems.

How did her passions feel when she became aware that his body was only an implement for her body, a seldom used implement?

She did not know me, but she knew about me. She knew he was having an affair with some other man. He had told her that many men, some of them were their neighbors, had affairs with other women. He had convinced her that this was more dangerous to a marriage than his outings. He did not refer to seeing me as being on a date; he did not speak to her about me, what we did or what we didn't do. If he needed to make any reference to Sunday evenings, he simply referred to our times together as his evenings out. He had convinced her that a husband is more stable if he is not chained down. She never forgot that he had told her before their marriage that he was bisexual and that he would not give up other men. They had agreed that he would have one evening out a week, but not the full night. What would the neighbors think if he came in at dawn? What would they think if he did not come home at all but went directly from someone else's bed to his office?

"I'm sorry she has to be put in the position of explaining anything, but I can't be the perfect married man. In my heart there is more perfection in our romance than in my marriage, yet I don't believe there is another couple in Brooklyn with a marriage as well adjusted as ours. Bill Thompson, who lives across the street from us, once said to me: 'Say, Terry man, you getting a little on the side?' I grinned his question away and said, 'You don't tell me everything, do you?' He laughed like a screwed hyena, and said, 'Oh man, if we told everything there wouldn't be a safe marriage in half of Brooklyn. But I will tell you this, my secretary, the one I have now, she is the hottest thing on two legs, or maybe I should say on her back.' He gave me the details of the affairs he had had with two out of three secretaries he had had since his marriage. 'And a little nookie here and there, just to keep in practice.' He said he didn't care a shot in hell about any of them, but he had to keep his balls from weighing him down to the ground."

"I thought of my love for you, Phillip. I am always thinking of my love for you, and I cannot see anything wrong in our love. I am not saying there is anything wrong with his little nookies here and his little nookies there, maybe his little nookies on the sly keep his marriage calm. Maybe his stolen freedoms keep him from feeling that marriage is a prison. He might run away from the prison if he did not have these breaks. Maybe they mean no more to his heart than a coffee break means to a secretary, but maybe they are just as necessary to get him through whatever he has to go through. My wife knows about Bill Thompson. Mrs. Thompson had left Bill the first time she realized it was happening, but she found out she was pregnant and went back to him. Mrs. Thompson told my wife she could do nothing but close her eyes to what was happening. 'But it's me he loves. I know, deep in his heart, it's me he really loves,' Mrs. Thompson had told my wife. And that was true before I met you. There were two other affairs since my marriage, and I loved them, but I knew I loved them less than I loved my wife. My love for you is more than an affair, our love is a romance. I try to hide the extent of my love for you from my wife, but there are times when I feel that she senses it. I feel the inside of myself drawing away from her. I respect her. In my way I respect her. She is the mother of my sons. The older one looks exactly like me, I can see it myself; he is a living mirror of myself. The youngest looks more like her. He has my eyes but her face. We combined ourselves and brought those two boys into the world. But now my world is you, Phillip. They live on the outer fringes of my life, there in the same house, our home, but they are not as close to me as you are, Phillip, even when we are apart. There is something about the spirit of our love that makes you so real to me, I sometimes reach out and touch you even though you are here in Manhattan and I am in Brooklyn.

"One night while I was getting undressed, I was standing near the open window and I reached my hand out – I felt you come to me in a slight summer breeze. My wife saw me and asked, 'What are you reaching for, Terry? There is no sign of rain, is there?' 'No,' I said. 'No sign of rain.' But I had left her, even though we were there in the same room. I touched you – you were in Manhattan, I was in Brooklyn. You seem to be in the air around me, and I breathe you. You overwhelm my life, Phillip. Our love transcends reality. There are times when I speak to my sons and I look at my sons and I see through them, as though they were transparent, and I see you. I see you and I feel you, no matter where I am, no matter who is with me. Your image is more realistic to me than the actual presence of others.

"I do not understand how I function on the job, but

apparently I am doing very well. I received another rise this past month. Maybe it is the power of your subliminal presence that enhances my abilities. That must be it. Seeing each other only once a week increases the power of my sublimated desire for you, and the power of my sublimated desire for you goes into my work. Freud made it clear years ago that sex can be a driving force in various realms of life. One afternoon one of my business associates barged into my office. With one hand I was writing a paper, a proposal for nationwide advertising, and with the other I was unconsciously caressing my crotch. The guy said, 'My God, Terry, you got a hard on like a firecracker about to explode. Careful or you'll have an orgasm all over that proposal.' I had not been consciously thinking about you, but my hand and my sex and my blood were feeling you. Sometimes I feel my cock has thoughts of its own. Yes, there is more power than sex in a man's genitals."

All these things he did not say in one evening. He said them through the weeks and through the months and through the years. I have gathered them here and put them together so that anyone may see the fullness of the man, a man who loved me in all the supreme beauty of love, a man, who later, felt the depths of torture.

Oh, my God up in Heaven, even to this very day I ask myself could I have possibly prevented that torture? Once it started, I do not know how I could have brought it to an end. But could I have prevented it from ever starting? If I had never known him, or if I had in knowing him never fallen in love with him or if he had never fallen in love with me, yes, in that way, his torture would have been prevented. But that is like saying if we were two other people we would not have lived the lives we lived. Of course we wouldn't. We would not have loved as we loved if we were not ourselves. The things of our lives would have been different, the events, the feelings. Hypothetical questions do not help any more than hypothetical answers. Such as saying: if Joe Blank and Jane Blank had never had any children they would not have been hurt by their children's drug addiction and subsequent deaths. A contraception on Joe Blank would have prevented the tragic death of the children who were never born. Try eating the seed of a peach instead of the peach itself. If Terry and I had never loved the subsequent torture would never have occurred. If you fail to be born, you fail to live.

So it is I cannot and do not regret my love for Terry Lane, nor do I regret his love for me. And the extent of his love? The depths and the breadth of his love? Need my conscience say to me in words to him: Terry, you should not have loved me so much, you should not have let your love for me pervade the atmosphere around you. You should not have let my spirit embrace you wherever you were, anywhere, anytime. Should my conscience be as cruel as all that?

That I should have given a single thought of putting limitations upon his love for me or my love for him, that would not have been me, that would have been another person; that he might have restrained his feelings for me, that would not have been Terry Lane. That would have been another couple, two other guys, two other men, another love affair, somebody else's romance.

We cannot rewrite our lives, life is not as easy as the writing of a book. Once you've lived a thing, you've lived it, and what is the good of regrets? Regrets are only little daggers of self-recrimination; regrets are needles of pain, sewing yourself to a past that cannot change.

And I would not change one thought of his love; I would not change one touch of his feelings, even if I could rewrite time, even if I could relive our lives.

As simple as it sounds, we are as we are.

We live, we die.

Why regret?

Chapter 9

WALTER AND VERA SMOTHERS...

Through those years, approximately eleven years I am writing about, remembering in the flow of my words, the years of an up and down and up again career which are detailed in another book and have no place here, the years which are detailed in everyone's life, the years, all our years are the legs of time walking around searching for the heart and the soul of life.

It was clear that Walter's heart and mind were in literature, and he gave his body to Vera. But where was Walter's soul? I know he believed he gave that to literature, also. He made a god of literature. But only whiffs and sprays of his soul invaded literature, and although the invasion conquered his mind and his heart, it never stilled his soul, the invasion did not give him peace. I doubt there was ever a man who found peace in the intellect, and Walter was nine-tenths intellectual and one-tenth all other essentials of life. What a brilliant fool he was! He was a fool because his brilliance was generally secondhand – what he learned he learned from books, lifting knowledge out of the mind of others. This, to some degree is commendable; it is an interaction of the mind, interrelations of the brain. Any man of knowledge must do this. But Walter yearned to write his own books. He never wrote them. He wrote at them. He would start a manuscript and he would drop it. It never lived up to his expectations. He had to be better than the best. Thus the results were nothing, with only bits and pieces scattered around the nothingness.

He could not go all the way.

His fears of not being the best destroyed his potentials as an author. He choked the life out of his creative desire, thus becoming non-creative, and gnawing upon the minds, the books, of others as though he were starving, even while he bulged with a belly full of intellect.

His search for knowledge glittered his mind, weighed upon his heart, and sometimes made him a pain in the ass.

Still I liked Walter, and I loved Vera with a friendship love. But I cannot honestly say I loved Walter with a friendship love. I admired him, yes, even when I wanted to ram my foot up his ass. But deep within himself, deep in the bowels of Walter, it was not a foot he wanted up there. Seven or eight inches would have been enough.

How much did Walter know about, or recognize, his desire for me? Or even his love for me? One of the reasons I liked him was because my ego very naturally appreciated his constant praise of my writings. He even wanted to write a book about me, even though I was not nearly famous enough.

He wanted to get me down on paper. How much of him sensed a more basic wanting? – He also wanted to get me down in the flesh with the flesh.

One evening while he and I were in the living room, and Vera was in the kitchen preparing dinner, his eyes fell upon my crotch and focused there. He was talking about Proust and Gide and Tennessee Williams and Truman Capote, and did not seem to realize that his eyeballs were trying to magnetically draw my balls out of my trousers. Those bubbles formed in the corners of his mouth.

Actually his eyes and those bubbles did those things in my presence several times, but that particular evening stands out in my mind, because I so clearly, too clearly, remember him saying, "I'd give my life to have what you have." He was talking about my creative spirit in the spoken word; his eyes were talking about my flesh in the unspoken words.

Perhaps I should have closed my legs but I didn't. I let his eyes have their way with me. I knew his mouth, his hands, his ass would not. He could not or would not go all the way. Just as he never finished a manuscript, he could not extend this desire to it's completion.

Upon reflection, I think it was slightly cruel of me to let myself become slightly erected.

He gasped. He covered his eyes with his hands, and said, "Oh, my God my God, I love, I love that, that book." He almost had to push the word "book" out of his mouth. We had been talking about *Remembrance of Things Past*.

He stood up and walked out to a window, and looking out and seeing only darkness, he said, "Those writers, yes, you, too, have something I'd give my life to have."

He was speaking of literature and feeling the pulsations of his blood in his veins, while still letting strings of his Southern soul cling to the restrictions of his strict upbringing...

The promiscuous man hits himself over his head with his phallus; the inhibited man stifles himself with an abundance of nothing.

It had become a friendly tradition for me to have dinner with Walter and Vera every Friday evening. Vera loved her duties as a wife and hostess. Walter took pride in being a magazine editor, and they both enjoyed entertaining people in the arts.

Others who came were:

Scott and Randy who had been lovers on and off for twenty years came when they were on-again. They never came separately. It was as if they were ashamed to show their faces to their friends when they were having a spat. Scott was a construction worker and Randy was a hairdresser. Scott would never have lifted a hand to Randy, but Randy had been known to viciously claw at Scott. They each wrote poetry and that is why Walter and Vera had become friends with them. Walter's magazine had published a few of Scott's poems – they were like delicate pieces of lace in the form of words. Randy's poems were cries against injustice, cries for equality for all. Fifteen years ago he had had one of his poems published in a Greenwich Village newspaper. Nothing since.

Janet and June were occasional guests on Friday evenings. Although they sometimes talked about their "boy friends", Walter, Vera and I believed they were technical virgins, repressed but attached lesbians. Janet was a nurse and June was a cab driver. They were artists, thus their reasons for being invited on these Friday evenings. No gallery or museum had ever shown their work and they had never sold a painting. Their technique was rather unusual – they worked on the same canvas simultaneously and you would not have known where Jane's brush strokes ended and Janet's began – the oils and the water colors blended together beautifully. Yet you could never see more than the surface of their paintings. The brush shied away from depth.

And there came sometimes, when he was not out cruising, delicate Dennis who had attempted suicide four times and had four ex-lovers. His tricks meant nothing, but oh my God how he loved those lovers almost unto death. He was not yet forty but dark circles were beginning to form under his eyes and tell the stories of his sad romances. He was much too quiet, but he could sometimes be persuaded to do an imitation of Marlene Dietrich singing "See What They Boys In The Backroom Will Have" or "Falling In Love Again." Falling in love again was his life story and if anybody knew what the boys in the backroom would have it was Dennis.

Walter told me about an evening when Vera was out grocery shopping and he and Dennis were alone in the apartment. Dennis had quite casually and gracefully but emphatically reached for Walter's crotch and offered to take care of everything he had.

"I was tempted," Walter said. "It popped up like a Jack-in-the-box, but I restrained myself. I thanked him kindly, begging off by being a married man. He's too fem. He's too much like a woman without being a woman. If I were going to do that sort of thing it would be with someone who, someone who... but of course I wouldn't." His voice trailed off wistfully.

It was a very rare thing for anyone to be there who was not gay or assumed to be gay. And they had to have some sort of artistic abilities or forget it. Who were they? What were they?

Walter was the one who gave the invitations. Vera did the shopping and cooking and serving. Since her man was the breadwinner, she did not seem to object to doing all these things. But I sometimes asked myself didn't she ever ask herself why all of Walter's friends were gay? Did she realize and understand that he gave vent to his own repressed homosexuality by surrounding himself with gay people? Did she realize her husband desired me? Did she realize her husband idolized me? Yet I don't think he loved me. He admired me, he envied me. Perhaps it was his envy of me that kept him from loving me. Envy and veiled resentments. I think he wanted to love me but did not know how.

She and I were alone one evening (Walter was in the bathroom having trouble with constipation – he held back everything) and she quoted a passage from Somerset Maugham which went something like this: "A man can live with a woman for ten years and not know the first thing about her." And she added, "A woman can be in the same situation. There is nobody I know better than I know Walter. But sometimes I think I don't know my own husband. Sometimes I start to ask a question, and he'll cut me off so sharply, it hurts. He doesn't mean to hurt me, but it happens anyway. I know him so well, but there is some part of him that is a blank. There is a deep dark well inside my husband and there is nothing I can do about it."

"Don't even try," I said. "Adjust to it."

"But he's my husband."

"He's still an individual. Even though two people may be united as one, they still have to respect each other's individuality." I paused. "Don't they?"

"I don't know. I suppose so. But I don't like that part of it. No, it's not so much I don't like it. I'm simply afraid of it. Afraid of his darkness. Afraid he'll fall down in that darkness and hurt himself."

Then she shrugged it off. Quickly. "Oh, but that's only now and then. Walter and I have the most beautiful marriage any man and woman could expect to have."

Walter came in on her last words, having, for the present, resolved his problem of constipation. "Of course we have. I've told you that many times."

On the surface one could easily see the beauty of their marriage. But way down in Walter there was something brewing, a simmering heat, claws that were outstretched, claws that were turned into themselves, balled up in a fist.

I do not know if Vera knew the meaning of those internal claws, but she did suspect something was in the darkness of her husband. She feared the darkness, but her fear was that of a Southern lady of gentility. As long as her husband lived she would have the utmost of respect for him; this would, of course, surpass and overshadow any feelings of fear.

One time I heard a man say, "The world is full of fear."

Walter's fear of his repressed desires and Vera's fear of the well of darkness in her husband are not exclusive to them. Walter sublimated these repressions in his love for the arts. Many men will strike out with their repressions, a fistful of repressions, and hurt the desires they cannot face. Others will drink themselves into a blackout and give vent to these "unmanly" desires and fail to remember anything when they become sober. Whether it is sex in the darkness of the night or sex in the darkness of one's mind, if a man does not release the depths of his desires, he is apt to turn against himself or overly praise himself. The man who is constantly bragging about his exploits with women may be the man who is deeply yearning for a boy, or another man, perhaps a man who will dominate him and force him to do what he wants but cannot admit to himself or another.

Walter talked round his desires: "If I were gay..." or "If I were that way..." If this and if that. Walter's tongue masturbated his great big *ifs*.

Vera thought it was wonderful that my romance with Terry Lane had lasted so many years. She understood how my creative spirit could, to some extent, make up for the absence of my lover during those six days and six nights.

Walter had long since given up making any objections to my affair with Terry, yet I knew he harbored resentments against it. The feelings that swirled around inside Walter or those that were ominously buried there would have filled a nice thick textbook. His intelligence and his emotions lived in different worlds of himself. I could see these two worlds. However, his wife lived somewhere between those worlds of Walter. She loved and admired one of his worlds; the other world of darkness frightened her and she generally pretended it did not exist. Surely she must have suspected these contents of that dark world, but I am sure she felt untrue to her husband if she lingered on any suspicions of him. Along with her love and obedience, she gave him her trust. She turned from the darkness and told herself it did not exist. She believed it was a wife's duty to trust her husband implicitly.

She loved the husband she knew, and if there was a fearful darkness in him, she must trust him over and beyond the darkness. That did not merely mean a bodily trust, that meant a trusting in and of the heart and mind too. I remember her saying to me: "He is the most tender lover any woman could ever expect to have."

I think if Walter had come out, he would have been a greedy lover, ravenous, insatiable, almost hungrily vicious.

Once I heard him say, "I, I just don't think I could do that sort of thing very well, I, I, I'm afraid my teeth would get in the way." I think his teeth would have wanted to get in the way.

It is amazing how much a man can shove into the darkness of himself.

Also, I believe if Walter had come out, and if he had chosen anal intercourse, he would not have given it to anyone, he would have rammed it to them, and teeth-marks would be on the back of his partner's neck.

Yet Vera had said he was the most tender lover a woman... a woman... how different a man can be with another man than he is with a woman.

He would have shot his load of emotions more forcefully than he could have shot anything else.

On one of those occasions when Vera had brought the matter up of not knowing her husband, I had said, "There are more people than we can count who walk around in darkness most of their lives. If they can manage not to break anything, they seem to get by."

Caring more about Vera than I cared about Walter, I hoped he would never break her heart.

She had already been terribly hurt by not having any children. They had tried for years with no results. She had gone to a doctor and been thoroughly examined. She was very fertile, and the doctor had indicated that it might be a good idea for her husband to be examined. Walter had flipped his lid and refused. He knew, "a man can tell" – nothing was wrong with him in that area.

I wanted to say to him that a man's ego can sometimes stand in the way of his life, but I kept my mouth shut. Preaching to your friends is one way of sending their friendship to hell. Walter was the sort of man who had to appear to have it all together; he could not let anyone know something was missing in his life; he would rather go without children than go to a doctor, admit to himself, his doctor, and his wife, there was even the remotest possibility that his seed were too weak to fertilize his wife.

So it was Walter's ego, rather than a contraceptive that covered his penis and kept them from having children.

Vera simply adjusted.

Chapter 10

I SHALL PIECE together a picture from the things he told me through the years, a picture of Terry Lane during the years before we met and loved and faced a tragedy together, a tragedy that left us face to face with a different life.

He had been attracted to men and women ever since he was a small child. During his time of puberty, when he played with the growing of himself, an image of a boy or a girl would come into his mind, and he never tried to figure out which he liked the most.

Let me tell you these things in his own words. His words come back to me in my memory, words to be scattered here as the scattered times of life are picked up by the reader and become a picture of the very young Terry Lane:

I was fascinated by both, boys and girls, and I was fifteen before these images turned into the real thing. I had, of course, seen other boys in the nude in the shower room at the beach, and wondered what it would be like to hold a fellow in my arms and feel his arms around me, and of course the wondering caused the rising of my desires. I would hold a towel in front of myself and pretend not to be looking at anyone, pretend there was something on the ceiling that interested me.

Then one day I saw another fellow who was holding his towel in front of him the same way I was holding my towel. And I realized he was hiding what I was hiding. My heart began to thump. He turned in such a way, the towel flared, and I saw briefly just a part of his erection. I swallowed and I clenched my buttocks, both at the same time. My eyes began to water. I became so excited I began to tremble and catch my breath. I thought my lungs were going to leave me. He set his eyes upon the towel in front of me. I wandered how he could be so bold. We heard someone coming and he looked the other way and turned around. The beauty of his buttocks caused me to sit down, I almost collapsed, on a bench.

The person we had heard passed on through the shower room.

The boy with the beautiful buttocks turned around and he looked me straight in the eye and that straight in the eye look made me know he was gay, even though I did not know the meaning of the word. Then he looked at my towel and pulled his towel aside, and smiled so alluringly, I automatically stood up and revealed my nakedness to him. The smile on his lips trembled. We were so stiff the tautness wanted to split our flesh. We knew each other's feelings. I did not know what to do about them. He did:

'I know a private spot over the dunes in the weeds,' he said, and I nodded my head. I was too choked up to speak.

We put on our bathing suits. They were terribly uncomfortable, holding down the stiffness of ourselves.

'Follow me,' he said.

So with our towels in front of us, hiding such intense desire we were in aching pain, we left the bath house.

'No,' he said. 'Maybe you shouldn't walk behind me. It'll look more natural if you walk beside me, pretending we're old friends, talking about something.'

'Talking about what,' I asked.

'I don't know, just anything. Did you ever do it with anybody before?'

'No, but I've thought about it lots and lots of times."

'I think about it so much, I can't sleep,' he said. 'I can't study. But you can't just think about it, you have to do something about it. It'll drive you crazy if you don't.'

'I don't know what to do with somebody else. Just by accident, just by fooling around with myself, I learned to do something to myself with my hands.'

'That's good. It's real good. But it's nothing compared to what I'll show you. I've got a brother, a year older than me, and he's got a friend a year older than him. And I walked in on them in the garage one day and caught them playing around. My brother yelled for me to get out, but the other guy, he's seventeen, he said no come on in and have fun together. He showed me what to do and I'll show you.'

'What?' I asked. I was anxious to know all about it.

'It's better to show you than to tell you. It's so much better than the hands all by yourself, you won't believe it. You think your scalp is gonna fly off, and you think your toes are gonna fall off, but nothing gets you together better than doing what I'm gonna show you. I think everybody ought to learn it.'

My flesh was crawling and quivering and trembling. Something way down deep inside myself was giving my flesh ideas my mind did not yet know how to formulate. So the boy from the shower room did not have too hard a time teaching me about what I wanted to learn.

When we came to the dunes, and he said, 'Strip off naked and spread your towel down,' I was already doing that before he told me.

As soon as I lay down he went down on me, and tears of bliss sprayed out of my eyes. I came too soon, but as I was coming, I felt as if my spine was melting away. It felt like my spine was turning to liquid, and he was drinking my spine. For a few flashing seconds, I felt as if every part of me was exploding and falling apart.

And he kissed me on my lips and I tasted the cream of myself, and I instantly liked the taste of myself, and it was while his lips were on my lips that I felt myself coming together again. It was like he had said.

His lips stayed on my lips for a while; then he whispered into my mouth:

'Lift your legs.'

'Why?' I asked. 'How?'

'I'll show you.'

My knees rose, and he reached down under my knees and helped me draw my bottom upwards. The stiffness and the heat of him probed at me and I felt the moisture of his pre-cum on my asshole, and although no one had ever told me this could be done, I instinctively knew what he was trying to do.

'I don't think I can,' I said. 'I think it's too tight.'

'It's never too tight.' he said.
'Mine is. I don't think I can. Oh, it hurts.'
'It only hurts until you learn to love it.'
The head of his stiffness was inside me.
'No, you can't, I can't. It hurts too much.'
'You're going to love it.'
And he sank deeper into me.
'You're splitting me apart.'
'You're going to love it.'
'I can't stand it.'
'You're going to love it.'
And by that time I was able to ask, 'Why does it feel so good and hurt so much all at the same time?'
'The hurt will go away and the good feeling will get even better.'
'When?'
'Let's do it lots.'
He nodded his head against my cheek. He could no longer talk. He had reached that point of ecstasy when the body encompasses the entire senses. His movements were an initiation into the basic movements of life, and when I felt the warm flow of his juice streaming inside me, that jet stream washed away all the pain.

He had opened up a new world for me.

That the opening between my buttocks could be a place of pleasure had never occurred to me. I thought it was for only something foul and ugly, but I had read somewhere that one of the purposes of art is to take the ugly and make it beautiful. We were only fifteen but we made it beautiful and beautifully.

We waited for a while. A breeze came along and rustled the tall grass around us. We lay in the nature of ourselves, and the nature of nature, and the nature of God.

I never felt there was anything wrong about it. I felt no trace of sin. I knew this was as much a part of me as breathing.

There was a world of nature right there with us. A gull made an ugly noise but I loved it. The stranger from the shower room had given me something I loved so much it caused me to love everything.

We needed only a short rest. Then we changed positions. I probed, and I made an exploration between his buttocks and I discovered a new world; I made new movements, and the warm summer breeze caressed my back and my shoulders, my buttocks and my legs, and as I made the upward movements, the breeze touched me between my buttocks while I delved between his.

I trembled in the intimate beauty of ourselves.

When I emptied myself into the tightness of him, I cried out and his lips caught my lips, and we trembled together.

I did not want to withdraw. Yet I wanted him. Suddenly I was so hungry for him, my tongue ached. I kept the connection; I let my tongue go down his chest and to his belly; he tightened his buttocks, and somehow I learned what is difficult to do – no one taught me; only the hungry nature of myself taught me: I went down on him while I was still inside him. He had taught me something new. And I had taught ourselves something new. As the intensity of my hunger grew, my buttocks began to make movements without my mind telling me what to do. Nature did the telling. Nature did the doing. As he began to flow into my mouth, I began to flow between his buttocks. Our bodies, our senses, timed ourselves.

I collapsed onto his chest, and as his legs fell, my penis limped out of him.

We let our breathing ease itself; we let our hearts beat more slowly.

There was a long silence... How could anything be so great, so wonderful, so beyond ourselves, yet from within ourselves? We did not expect spoken answers to the unasked questions. Our flesh was the answer.

But he did ask: 'How did you learn to do that? I thought I was teaching you something new. But oh geez, when you did me while you were still inside me, I just didn't think I could stand it.'

'Nobody taught me. It just felt like the natural thing to do.'

I don't remember how we parted. I had forgotten to ask his name, and he had not asked mine. We simply didn't think about it. Many times after that I wished I had known how to contact him, but we never saw each other again. Still I have never forgotten him, and I hope he remembers me.

Then it was only a week later that the sister of my brother's friend came to our house looking for him. I was on our back porch and I saw her go into the garage at the back of our house. I knew she was looking for her brother, but I did not know I was looking for a new experience in my life. Yet my flesh remembered that the boy who first seduced me was first seduced in a garage. Our flesh sometimes knows more than our mind permits us to know. Just as if the flesh was telling my mind what to do, instead of my mind telling my flesh. I went out to the garage to tell her that her brother was not there.

That was one Saturday afternoon a long time ago.

The garage was in semi-darkness. She was wearing blue jeans. Her hair was cut a little short. She was wearing her brother's shirt, and it was open to the center of her bosom. A part of her brassiere was showing, as though it were lace upon a mystery. Her breasts were not large, but they were not small either. They were just large enough to make me wonder about them. She was a year younger than her brother, a year older than me. She was sixteen.

The car was not in the garage. All sorts of things, junk my mother called them, were stored in the back of the garage. When I entered the garage she was staring at the stack of stuff as if it might contain the crown jewels, as well as snakes and rats and toads. She turned her gaze at me when she heard me come in. We simply stared at each other for a minute or so. This was not the first time we had seen each other, but it was the first time we were alone. I don't know why we let the silence linger. It was not an uncomfortable silence. It was a penetrating silence. We liked what we saw. We were enjoying the sight of each other. Yes, I suppose that is why the silence lasted so long. She was very pretty. She was not beautiful. She did not need to be. I did not think of the stranger on the beach. My blood, before my mind, simply wondered what it would be like to suck her breasts.

Her words came into the silence, softly: 'If I had lots of money, I would go to the jewelry store, and see if I could buy a couple of emeralds as green and beautiful as your eyes.'

'Thank you.'

My sex began to rise.

'Do you think I'm being fresh saying that? Actually I'm looking for my brother.'

'He's not here. He rode off with my brother. Somewhere. I don't knew where.'

'Why are you staring at me that way?'

'I can't help it.'

'If your eyes weren't so beautiful, I would resent the way you are looking at me.'

'Don't resent it.'

'I'm not resenting it. Maybe I should. But I don't.'

'I'm glad.' I moved a little closer.

'Did you ever practice hypnotism?'

'No.'

'Your eyes are now. There ought to be a law against anybody's eyes being so green and beautiful,' she said.

'Would you have me arrested, if there were such a law?'

'No.' She paused. Then she said, 'I would help you break the law.'

As if my body were wired to do so, I turned and closed the garage door behind me.

'Why?' she asked. 'Why did you do that?'

'Don't we know? Isn't it natural?'

'Yes. I guess so.'

'It has to be.' I was close to her, almost touching her.

A slender stream of light was coming in through a small window in the garage. I could see her eyes. I saw no rejection there. I knew she was seeing my eyes. 'I like nature,' I said. 'Do you?'

'I've heard about it. Human nature.'

'Human nature,' I echoed.

We embraced. We kissed. The kiss lingered. I felt her breasts against my chest. I knew she was feeling my sex against her belly.

The quivering of her body in my arms first strengthened the kiss, then loosened our lips, as she said, 'I've never done it. I don't know if we should. I don't want to have a baby.'

'I'll take it out just before I come. Let it fall on your belly.'

'I don't think any jewellry store could possibly have

emeralds as beautiful as your eyes.'

'That is the way she gave her consent.'

I don't know how I knew, but I knew there was an old quilt, a Dutch Doll quilt my mother called it, there in that junk at the back of the garage. It did not take me long to find it, and by the time I found it she was undressed. And then it was I thought of the stranger on the beach. I was fascinated by the difference. For me, there was not just one world – there were two worlds to explore, and I knew instinctively that I would explore both worlds over and over again.

I tossed the Dutch Doll quilt down onto the floor of the garage, and while I was getting undressed, she straightened out the quilt.

She was sitting on the quilt, I was standing over her. 'Why does it stand up like that all by itself?' She asked.

'Nature,' I said. 'I love nature.'

'Nature,' she said. 'I guess everybody should know about nature, sooner or later.'

I stood there for a few seconds while she gazed at it, thinking she might want to take it in her mouth, but then I realized she did not want it that way. So I sat down on the quilt and gathered her up in my arms. My mouth instinctively went to her breasts, from one breast to the other. It was overwhelming that she had two of them. Suppose the stranger on the beach had had two cocks, they would have driven me out of my mind. My mouth wanted to be everywhere at once. From her breasts to her lips, to her throat, and to her breasts again.

Nature revealed itself in an abundance of joys.

I entered her, and there is no more beautiful cry than the cry of a girl while her hymen is being broken. At least to me, it is even more – what shall I say – intriguing, satisfying to the male ego than the cry that is heard while penetrating the male anus; it is as if an unseen banner is waving, and imprinted upon the banner is Hail, the *Conquering Hero Comes*, or maybe the testicles are always weaving such a banner during intercourse, but the breaking of the hymen seems to emphasize the Hail, the *Conquering Hero Comes* feeling.

Her legs embraced me.

Her movements were in rhythm with my movements.

We discovered the pains of passion between male and female. I wanted to go deeper and deeper, but the root of me was as deep inside the suction cup of her as flesh and flesh could be joined. The burning seas of the internal world rocked within us. Our blood seemed to exchange vessels in which to flow.

I do not know if my eyes had in any way hypnotized her. I do know that with her and with the stranger on the beach, and with many others, and especially with you, Phillip, I am hypnotized by passion. It is as if an interlocking, interlacing, intermingling, of hypnotism occurs.

Her name was Lydia.

I don't think a man ever forgets his first time with a girl or a woman.

I shall never forget Lydia.

And I'll never forget that stranger on the beach, and how much I ached to be with him again. I went to the beach that summer every chance I had, but I never saw him again.

I suppose many so-called straight guys forget their first experiments in sex with another boy or man. They forget because they haven't the courage to remember. They forget because they are afraid of it. I never feared sex. I always knew it was something to give my body freedom. And I have been free with it.

Lydia and I saw each other once a week for nearly two years. We broke it off simply because she became engaged to be married. Nobody's heart was broken, nobody hurt anybody.

But all during those two years, even though I was having regular sex with Lydia, I was also having sex with other guys around my same age and grown men too.

I had discovered a park near the Court House, and it wasn't long before I learned that it had an underground reputation of being a gay park. I remember one of the men who picked me up was a man in his late forties whose wife was in the hospital having their seventh baby. He took me to his office in the Court House. He just happened to be a judge. I liked the kind of judgement he passed on me.

Since I could not have the stranger on the beach again, I wanted as many new strangers as I could find. Believe me, I found them, if they didn't find me first. Sometimes we did it right there in the park, in the bushes or behind a big tree. If we soiled the knees of our trousers, we simply didn't care. One time my mother asked why I so frequently had dirt stains or grass stains on the knees of my trousers. So a quick lie came to me about there being some new kind of ball game where you could not catch the ball standing up, you had to catch the ball kneeling down. 'What a strange kind of ball game,' she commented. Maybe there is a strange thing about gay strangers – we become so familiar so quickly. I caught hundreds of balls in that kind of ball game. As long as I was seeing Lydia, I did not seek out another girl, but I cruised one guy after another. After what Lydia had said about my eyes hypnotizing her, I used my eyes to make pick ups. But of course pick up eyes are not unique in gay life. I could just glance at a guy in that gay park, blink my eyelashes, and he would move a little closer, sometimes caressing the edge of his crotch as he came nearer. However, I learned there was a type who did not want me. I was a clean cut kid, but there were those who did not want to have anything to do with me. They wanted rough trade or they wanted the down-and-outers, sloppy guys or what was called butch. I was never butch and I certainly was never fem. I think I was and am just a normal guy who goes for men and women. Both were in the plural until I married. But after Lydia and I parted and before my marriage whenever I went with a girl, one girl was enough. Still I wanted as many guys as I could get. Until I met you, Phillip. I've never wanted another guy since that first time with you, and then my desire for my wife soon began to fade, until it has now faded away. There is left only my respect for her as the mother of my sons.

... Again, these things he told me through the years, not altogether as I have written them down there where my memory touches memory...

I cannot believe, regardless of what happened later, I shall never believe he lost respect for his wife. There are those who may ask, how could he have sexual relations with other men if he truly respected his wife. It was his nature as a bisexual, an overt bisexual, not one, as are so many, who repress or sublimate one on the other side of his nature. He knew why nature had created his erotogenic zones – his mouth, his anus, his genitals. He was the most complete man I have ever known. He was superb.

I loved him enough to share him with a woman, to be grateful for, to be thrilled with only one-seventh, less than one-seventh of his time. So if I were a woman (and even though I do not feel effeminate, this is not too difficult to imagine), I believe I would have loved him enough to share him with other men. If I were she, I would have recognized this and loving him so much, I would have accepted this as a part of his nature. I, his male lover, could not give him children. But he had a definite paternal instinct which I could not satisfy. That part of his nature he had to have; it belonged to him. If God gave me the paternal instinct, he gave me only a little of it, and I thank God I have no children. I know that Terry Lane was grateful to God, to his wife and to himself for his two sons.

So it was that in certain ways we were very different. I respect our differences. Our love gave us this respect. The love that existed between he and his wife must have given her the recognition that his desire for men could not or would not be extinguished by her love. She must have known either consciously or subconsciously that if she had tried to extinguish that other love, she would have extinguished his love for her and driven him away.

I do not know exactly when his love for his wife began to diminish, perhaps infinitesimally from the very beginning of our romance, and then slowly, slowly faded into dutiful sex with her, faded till there was no real desire, but only respect. Yes and I write that phase "only respect" it does not seem accurate. Respect is a beautiful feeling, much too rarely exercised, not only between people in general, but respect is also too rarely felt between husband and wife.

How did she feel when she realized he no longer desired her and did not really want to share with her anything except his respect for her and to be hers as the father of her children.

I think there must have come an emptiness into the pit of her belly. Maybe she occasionally let a tear fall in silence where he would not see the tear. He would have told me of her tears if he had seen them. Hopefully she had enough pride in being the mother of his children that it alleviated or blanked out any ache in her heart.

I do not doubt that she went on loving him.

I cannot blame myself. I cannot blame him. Nor do I blame her for any of her feelings. I do not care to cast stones. It is simply that life is complicated. Any one human being is filled with a world of feelings. Some of the feelings never come forth. Yet at another time, some sort of feeling may burst forth in an abundance of unsealed, uncapped vibrations, and ignite an otherwise peacefully accepted situation.

I do not believe I was ever really jealous of her, but I am glad I never met her. I am glad he never showed me a photograph or even a snapshot. In my mind's eye, she remains a mist in the background. I have even forgotten her name. That is why it never appears anywhere here in these memories of him. He usually referred to her as his wife or the mother of his sons. "My son's mother" or "Their mother."

Only once did he show me a snapshot of his two sons. At the time, one was twelve, the other thirteen. The oldest looked enough like him to have been a picture of himself. The youngest resembled their mother, except for the eyes, the eyes were the eyes of Terry Lane. For a moment an image of his wife came through to me from the snapshot of the twelve year old child. I flicked the image away. She did not seem to be real. She z lived in a foreign world. I did not need any thoughts of her. I let her be nothing to me. I could not imagine her being intimate with Terry. On the other hand, it was easy for me to imagine his sons entering puberty.

"They are beginning to discover themselves," Terry said as he showed me their snapshots.

"How do you mean?" I knew what he meant. I wanted to hear him say it.

"I walked in on them one day and I caught them playing with each other's pricks."

"Did you say anything? Did they?"

"'Oophs' I said and closed the door. Then I realized there had been a slight expression of fear in their faces when they saw me. So I opened the door and said, 'Enjoy yourself, fellows'."

"Do you think they are gay? Either of them?"

"I don't know. I hope they will be like me. I hope they will be bisexual. But that, of course, is up to them. Do you ever feel like you've missed some part of your life by not having children, Phillip?"

(I was thirty-three when he asked this question.)

"No. My books are my children."

"So long as you are satisfied," he said.

We wanted for the other what the other wanted.

I would not have wanted to take anything away from him. He would not have wanted me to have anything I did not want. He was my life, but not my whole life. Literature, my creative spirit, the arts were another world for me. I knew two worlds. I lived in a world of romance; I lived in the world of the arts.

And there was that general world out there somewhere, either being beautiful or making a fool of itself. Korea came along somewhere during our romance, but we were exempt because we had known the Second World War. McCarthyism passed wind upon the freedom of Americans, but we could do nothing about McCarthy's bowels.

So much of the time we were so much into each other, we could leave the outside world to itself. Our own world of love was too beautiful for intruders. There was too little time in our nine hours a week to permit those other worlds to come into our minds, and certainly not into our hearts.

I could spend an hour or more, wordless, with my cheek serenely resting upon his belly, gazing quietly at the glittering gold of his blond pubic hair. Unarousingly caressing him. Softly, softly, till the time of arousing arose of its own accord. And his flesh itself told me to take him again.

I drank from the Fountain of Love. My internal being wore a liquid coating of my beloved.

We were the mingling of ourselves.

We were the interlacing of our internal beings.

We knew the quiet, rushing thunders of love, and we knew the stillness of love.

Chapter 11

AND THEN IT was after a little more than eleven years of our romance, nine hours of paradise per week, approximately five thousand hours together, spread across those years, and then it was the power and the cruelty of tragedy came into our lives, disrupting our lives, changing the course of beauty, as though a beautiful stream had been streaming through a meadow and there came an earthquake and the meadow disappears and is being swallowed into the bowels of the earth, and from the broken earth there gushes up the fires of wrath and the rocks and the stones and sharp little pebbles fall where the meadow had once lain and had known the flowing stream, where now there was the muddy waters of disrupted time.

Let me say again, let me see it again in the written word, here before my eyes: I cannot blame Terry Lane, I refuse to blame myself, and I cannot blame her.

Let me share these turmoils of life with you as I have shared the beauty and the bliss of love with you; let me ease the remembrance of pain in the sharing of it with you, setting it down before you in the written word, and allowing you to think whatever thoughts you want to think. Judge us. Forgive us. Think of us as you may. I simply want to tell it to you and let the telling of it ease the memory, for now, at this hour, the memory of the tragedy is clawing at the memory of our bliss together, so that I may keep foremost in my memory the beauty of our love.

It is through the years that I have learned that we must not permit tragedy and cruelty and pain to linger in the forefront of our lives. We all have to go through it some time or other, some way or other, but we must, and this I have learned through the years, we must not give adversity the upper hand of our lives, neither in the living of life nor in the memory of it. We must face and then cleanse it from our minds, cleanse it from our hearts and our souls, else the spirit of life becomes an evil spirit, plaguing us in all that we do through all our days and through all our nights.

Terry Lane called me in the middle of the night, that night of the tragedy. I remember it was exactly half past two in the morning, late Monday night or early Tuesday morning.

"Phillip, Phillip, I must talk to you." I had never heard this sound of alarm in his voice; there was fear and sadness and anguish. "I can't believe what has happened. It can't be true. It's horrible."

"Tell me," I urged him.

"I...I, I can't talk on the phone. The phone is so cold."

"Tell me, Terry."

"No. Please. You come to me," he said.

"But your wife?"

I had never been to his home in all the eleven years we had been lovers. I did not even know his address; all I knew was that he had a private home in Brooklyn.

"Never mind her." There was a strange cry in his voice.

"Give me your address, Terry. I'll be there as soon as possible."

"But don't you know? You come here to me so much of the time. No, of course you don't know. I'm confusing dreams and reality. I've just had a nightmare."

He sounded as if he were wandering around in his mind, disconnected. The tone of his voice frightened me, but I knew I had to keep it cool, keep my head on my shoulders. He needed me obviously in a way he had never needed me before. The cry in his voice came to me through the telephone wires and pained my heart.

"Give me your address, Terry."

"Oh, yes, yes," he sounded dizzy, but he managed to give me the name of the street on which he lived and the house number.

"Take it easy, Terry. I'm coming."

We hung up.

I always slept in the nude, and there I was stark naked with a hard on while he was in the midst of something horrible. Does passion exceed tragedy? My mind raced. Should I call a cab or should I take a subway train? Which was faster? Is the blood of desire stronger than a nightmare in your lover's life? There would be little traffic at this time of night. I called a cab while I was pulling on my briefs, wearing the erection up under my briefs, thinking of Terry Lane in my arms, worrying about what had happened, the thoughts jumbled around inside me, the passion and the worry. I dressed as quickly as possible. And by the time I was fully dressed and went downstairs, the cab had arrived and was parked in front of my apartment house.

I gave the driver the address in Brooklyn. The cab driver was the talkative kind; my erection limped away. I don't remember what the cab driver was talking about. It didn't matter. He was the type who talked just to hear himself talk. I grunted my answers. My mind was in Brooklyn with Terry. My mind was filled with questions. I was in a blank world. My heart began to race with fear. I must not let the fear get the upper hand of me. Terry Lane was my lover, my lover needed me. He would need my strength. He would need my courage. He would not need my fears. I must be calm. I must share a strong heart of love with him, not a racing heart. In all these years I had never been to his home; he had never called me to him. He had always come to me, never missing a single Sunday in all those eleven years. Years of love, years of passion. Think of these years, our years. Do not think of the tone of tragedy in his voice. Go to him and wipe the tragedy away, cleanse it out of his life. What are the children doing? No. Do not think about his children. But they are a part of him. Where is his wife that he should call me to come to his home? Has she gone away? Has she left him? Have they had an argument and she has demanded to meet me, to confront me? That did not sound logical? Why? Why not? Do not think about his wife. Do not think about his children. Do not think about the unknown tragedy, or that tragic frightened tone in his beloved voice. Think about his beauty. Think about the smoothness of his flesh. Think about the innumerable times he has spoken to me of his love for me. Think about the power of his penis, the strength of his jaws, the depths between his buttocks. Why doesn't the cab driver drive faster? Why did he miss that green light? Is he having a winking love affair with red lights? Think about the red ruby of flesh that burns upon my lover's rod of romance. Let my thoughts flow with the cream of love. Still the racing of the mind. Ease the beating of my heart. What in heaven's name has happened to disturb my lover's peace of mind? Should I throw the cab driver out, steal his cab, drive upon the sidewalk and race around that cab in front of us? My mind and my heart are going faster than the wheels of his damn cab. Ease myself. Calm myself. His kisses in the aftermath are like breezes of summer travelling across my flesh, caressing into me memories to tide me over from one Sunday evening till the next Sunday afternoon. This is late Monday night, no, early Tuesday morning. It is nearly three-thirty, a little after three-thirty in the morning, and we must be nearly there. He can't be far away now. I want to hold him in my arms; I want to crush out whatever it is that is bothering him.

We came to a street where there were no apartment houses, only private homes, unattached, with honest-to-God front yards and even breathing space between the houses. I managed to catch a glimpse at the street on which the driver crept along; yes, it was the street on which Terry lived. We were coming closer to the number of his house. My money was out of my pocket. The driver stopped. I gave the driver some bills; I overpaid or over-tipped, and I jumped out of the cab.

Terry was standing there, waiting, on his front porch.

I heard the cab drive away.

I started to run, then I caught myself, held down my anxiety and walked rapidly to him.

His hands grabbed my upper arms; my hands held his elbows.

He opened his mouth to speak; no words came out.

The green of his eyes had darkened. His lips trembled, not in passion as I had known them to tremble for me, but in fear.

"What is it, Terry?" I heard myself speaking in a dense whisper.

Again he tried to speak. Tears came into the corners of his

eyes, and they were not the tears of overflowing joys of love, they were the tears of sadness in his fear. No word came from him.

"I love you, Terry. I am here. I am with you."

His head fell against my chest. Muffled cries of despair came from him. I swallowed, as though I were swallowing down my own tears. I caressed his shoulders; I caressed the back of his neck. Dry sobs shook him.

"Easy, easy," I whispered. "Let it out, let it out, easy."

Gently I led him over to the swing there at the end of the porch. For a fleeting second I saw an image of his sons swinging there in the swing. Where was his wife? I did not ask.

There was a tiny pink light near the door that revealed the house number. The swing was in the darkness. A curtain of ivy was growing up over that end of the front porch bannister, all the way to the roof. We were secluded. There were hardly any stars. The moon was slender.

I sat him in the swing as I sat down beside him, close to him, touching him. His hands were grasping at mine as if he would strip the flesh off my hands and cover the bones of his hands.

"Easy, Terry."

He was grasping me as though he were trying to draw strength, courage, from out of me to give himself the ability to speak.

"I love you, Terry. I love you with all my heart."

And then the words gushed from him in a quiet and trembling cry: "Oh, my God, Phillip, I love you, I love you, I've loved you too much. Phillip, Phillip, I did not mean to love you so much. How was I to know? How was I to know?"

His head was on my shoulder. I caressed the side of his forehead with my chin.

"We have a right to our love," I tried to reassure him. "Know what, Terry?"

"How was I to know she was killing herself inside herself? I never intended to be cruel. I had to be myself. I told her before we were married, yes, I told her, I told her I was bisexual. She seemed to accept me for myself. She never complained about our Sunday evenings. Now it seems as if all these years she has been burying down little daggers inside herself, sharp little stones of tears, tears she never cried. I could not help myself last night."

He paused. There was a deep shuddering silence, as if he had talked himself into a deep cake of ice. The heart of his anguish turned cold.

I kissed the top of his head, his silk blond hair. I held him close to me there in the darkness on the porch. I tried to give him the courage to pour it out. I glanced up through the ivy into the sky – the tips of the new moon appeared to be as sharp as knives.

"Through the years, Phillip, I believe I mentioned it to you only now and then, my desire for her simply faded away. I've known of it happening to other married couples. The honeymoon does not last forever. Yet ours, yours and mine, Phillip, ours has increased in depth and love. So deep, Phillip, so deep that I grew blind to what was going on inside her. I fell in love over my head, Phillip. Phillip, Phillip, I love you so much I became half blind toward the rest of the world."

"Please don't blame our love for anything, Terry. Whatever has happened, don't blame our love."

"No. I can't blame our love. No. Not our love. Some part of me, the married part, became blind, no, not completely blind, only half blind. She hid her feelings from me, perhaps she hid them from even herself. Maybe she did not know she was in pain. Or maybe she knew only too well. I suppose an invisible cloud was growing between us, my wife and I. Something strange was and we did not know what it was. Yet, I knew I was loving you more and more as the years went along. I knew I desired her less and less. But I never lost my respect for her as the mother of my sons."

He paused again, as if he were seeing his sons growing through the years. The eldest had been five when Terry and I met; now he was sixteen.

I intruded upon his silence. "Where are your sons now, Terry?"

"Sleeping," he answered, speaking slowly. "It was all very quiet. They have slept through it all. They are sleeping, sleeping. What will happen when they awake?"

"Slept through all of what, Terry?

He pressed his head upon me as though he would sink into my shoulder, as though he would hide himself beneath my skin, disappear from this time of trouble, and become his lover-myself, rather than himself.

"The nightmare," he spoke in pain.

"The nightmare?"

He lifted his head slightly, and let his words speak into my neck, seep into my throat: "We had been together again, you and I, Sunday evening on another trip to paradise. It seemed to me at the time, and afterwards too, that we had gone beyond ourselves; we achieved heights beyond all other heights; we were sublime; we were transported into each other and into another realm of existence. I remained in that state of mind until, until the nightmare. I did not want to come out of the beauty of you, the beauty of us; I did not want to come out of the exalted state of mind. Yesterday, Monday, all day at the office, I was in another world. I heard people talking, but they were not in my world. I conducted my business reasonably well, but I was not in my real world. I was in the world of us, Phillip, the world of you and me, and our world of bliss, our heaven."

He paused for a long time. I did not intrude upon the pause. I relished the silence of ourselves, remembering that I, too, had been transported into the same paradise of which he spoke, for we had created the paradise together.

When he came out of the golden silence, he said: "But then last night, no, early this morning, after midnight, she woke me, trying to stir me up. She had her hand on my genitals; she was trying to arouse me. Suddenly I felt disgusted. Her hand felt clammy. She was trying to crawl on top of me. I thought, maybe I didn't even think, I only felt, felt too much the feelings of disgust, felt she was trying to take me away from you. A wave of raging wrath swept through me. I had never felt such a feeling in all my life. The wrath pushed her off me, and I was half on her, still half asleep, half in a nightmare, half in a distorted reality. 'Bitch! Bitch!' I hissed those horrible words into my wife's face: 'Don't ever touch me again!' My hands went to her throat. But something restrained me. I did not squeeze. My knuckles froze in the dead heat of wrath. I don't think I even touched her throat. I was not myself, Phillip. I was not the man you know, Phillip. I was a monster of unrestrained rage. I was not the man she had married. I was someone else. For a few seconds I wanted to kill her. I would have killed her if my innate sense of decency had not restrained the monster inside myself. I jarred myself. I became fully awake. I do not claim to have been asleep, but some part of me was seeped in something like a nightmare. I realized what I was doing, even though I did not understand that part of me. I caught myself. The rigidness of myself loosened up. I let go of her. 'I'm sorry,' I said. 'That was not me. Forgive me. I did not mean what I said.' Then it flashed into my mind: give her what she wants. Have sex with her. But I knew I couldn't. I did not even try,. I was as limp as a cold worm. I felt empty. 'Forgive me,' I said again. She was quiet for a moment. I lay on my back looking at the ceiling; I could feel her in the same position, as if we both thought the ceiling would come down and wipe it away. Wipe away those few moments, only a few moments. But I suppose, yes, I am sure, those few moments came from the years, years of drifting apart, even while sleeping side by side.

"She cut the silence with a whisper of false warmth. I sensed something false about her tone, but what she said made sense. 'Let's not ever mention it again. I think what I need now is a warm bath, a bubble bath. It will quiet my nerves.' She sat up. She looked at me through the darkness of the room. We could not see each other clearly. But we saw. She lifted her hand as if to touch me on my chest, my heart. But she drew her hand away, without touching me, as if the hand remembered my words – *don't ever touch me again*. If I had grabbed her hand in my hand and kissed her hand if I had, if I had... but I didn't. I couldn't. My own wrath had frozen me. I lay in a vacuum of myself. She sensed the vacuum. She was aware of my frozen heart. I had not intended for it to freeze against her. The mother of my children. I think she had gone on believing, some part of her maybe doubting, but some part of her believing she was not just the mother of our children but my wife, not the discarded wife, of the man she had married over eleven years ago.

Believing until, until I said those terribly cruel words, knifing her in her heart with a tongue I never intended to use as a knife.

"She crept out of bed. Then she lifted up her shoulders as she slipped into a lovely lace neglige and left me. She went into the bathroom. I could hear the water running. I don't believe the boys heard anything. Their room is at the other end of the hallway and they sleep like a couple of logs. Then I felt the silence after the running of the water. I could imagine her pouring the bath salts into the water. I could imagine her slipping out of the neglige and hanging it behind the bathroom door. I could imagine her stepping into the tub of warm water – she liked it very warm – and sinking under the bubbles up to her chin. I had seen her do these things many times. A simple bubble bath. For relaxation. I tried to wipe my cruel words out of my thoughts: *Bitch! Bitch! Don't ever touch me again.* It was not only the words. It was the way I viciously hissed the words. My hands going to her throat and freezing only a quarter of an inch, only an eighth of an inch, away from her throat. Some part of me wanting to choke her. Some part of me, a part I did not know existed, wanting to kill her. I tried to wipe these things out of my mind. I twisted. I turned. It was hell. I got up and I went over to the open window, and I tried to bring the spirit of you, Phillip, I tried to bring your spirit to me. I've done it before. I've told you about it. Loving you so much, bringing your spirit to me, feeling the vibrations of you in the atmosphere. But I could not bring you to me. Something blocked the spiritual connection. The thing that had happened with my wife caused too much negativity in the atmosphere – it threw up a shield and kept your spirit from me. I felt drained. And I never felt more lonely in all my life. Then something happened in the pit of my stomach while I stood there trying to make spiritual contact with you. My belly sank down inside me; my balls tightened in a weird fear. I felt a slight nausea. A cold chill, even in the warmth of the night, a cold chill swept over me.

Then I realized she was taking an interminably long time in the bubble bath. Yet it was not so much the length of time that bothered me. It was the feeling of the time, as if time stopped, and then decided to pass on away and out of existence. I was wrenched out of myself and away from the window. I do not know if I ran or if I crept out of the bedroom, down the few steps of the hallway to the bathroom. She had not locked the door. We seldom ever locked the bathroom door because we usually knew who was in the bathroom. I went in, but I did not see her. I stood still just inside the doorway. I could not believe what I saw, but I had to believe it. The water was red and there was a reflection of red in the bubbles. I clenched my jaws painfully. I went over to the tub. She had slit her wrist. She had sunk under the water. I could see her only dimly in the water. I had never imagined her being dead. She did not look real. I stared at her, not believing what I saw. The silence made a grave of the bathroom. There was a weird beauty in the color of the water. Pink, reddish reflections in the bubbles. A bubble bath of death. I was in a trance of disbelief. I did not know what to do. My mind went blank. It seemed to have fallen down into the empty pit of my stomach. My heart was still. Then you came into my mind, Phillip. I had to call you. I had to see you. I had to feel your touch. I think I choked some part of my life out of me when I almost, without my fingers touching her, almost choked her. She could not endure the kiss of my wrath, those few fleeting moments of hatred. Fleeting moments of hatred that did not flee away but sank into her bloodstream. She had slit her wrists with one of my razor blades. I saw the box of Gilette razors there on the seat of the toilet. It had been quick, almost painless, physically. But emotionally she had felt the wrath of hell when she heard my wrath. Maybe she had lived in a quietly accepted hell for years, pretending to be the open-minded modern wife. My wrath shattered her pretensions."

My lover trembled in my arms there in the front porch swing behind the ivy.

"Phillip. Phillip. I killed her without touching her. That is the way I killed her, by not touching her. And it was because I did not want her to touch me. Not ever again. And now. She'll never reach for me again. I killed her, Phillip."

"No," I said, and I tried to make my voice sound firm. "Get that thought out of your head. You did not kill her. You haven't called the police, have you?"

"No. I couldn't think what to do."

"We'll have to call them."

"I can't call them."

"I'll do it for you. There'll be questions. Some of the questions may be sticky, Terry. Get hold of yourself. I'd better call them now. Then we'll think of what to say when the police come. Where is the telephone?"

"In the living room, near that large chair to your right as you go in."

"Wait here, Terry. Try to relax. Breathe in deeply and slowly. Let the air out slow and easy. That will help you to relax. Try. Try to take it easy."

I went into the living room, fumbled for the light switch of a lamp, and I called the emergency number 9ll, and told the police there had been a suicide. I let them know I was a friend of Mr. Lane's. He was too shaken to make the call himself.

While I was on the phone, only briefly, I thought I had heard a sound upstairs. Then just as I placed the receiver on the hook, I heard a scream, loud and long: *"Mama! No! Mama! No!"*

The scream pierced down the stairs, choked my throat and pained my heart.

Terry heard it from outside. He came running in and up the stairway.

What in God's name will he tell his sons? How can I help him? Yes, of course, he should have told them before one of them saw her there in the red bubble bath. But never mind the *shoulds* and the *shouldn'ts* of life. Never mind the *shoulds* and *shouldn'ts* of death. They always come up in the face of death. If I, if we, had done or said such and such, would so and so be alive today? Could we have saved someone else some of the pain? If, if, if – yes, if we had known how.

I walked up the stairs slowly, not even knowing if I should reveal myself to his sons. But now I must be the friend of the family – the father's friend very naturally being a friend to the family, even though I had never met his sons, even though I had never seen his wife.

Before I had reached the top of the stairs the eldest son came out of his bedroom and was rushing to the bathroom where he heard the sounds of grief, the sounds of tragedy. I knew the youth was Terry Lane, Jr. because the instant I saw him I remembered Terry's description – he was a sixteen year old replica of his father, my lover.

It had been the youngest son who had seen their mother and cried out.

I went to the door of the bathroom, and I heard Terry speaking to the sons, "Don't look at her. Try not to look."

But the eldest son was staring at the tub of reddish pink bubbles, then at his father, then at me.

"I can't believe it. It can't be true," I heard him say. Then I saw Terry draw him to his side and press his head on one side of his chest, and he was pressing the head of the youngest son against the other side of his chest. The younger son – what was his name, Ronald? – yes, Ronald was his name – Ronald was sobbing uncontrollably, but Terry, Jr. was taking the tragedy in cold disbelief. He did not weep. He did not sob. I could see unshed tears swimming in unbelievable grief in his eyes as he kept saying, "It can't be true."

Ronald must have sensed the presence of another person. He lifted his head from his father's chest and glared at me, and his voice shot out at me in a sharp blaze of hatred: "Did you kill my mother?"

Did I?

Of course not!

I merely loved her husband. I merely loved your father.

A wave of pain swept around and through my heart. My spine tingled. I felt sweat between my buttocks.

I saw a new pain in Terry's eyes as he glanced at me when he heard his son ask his lover if I had killed his mother.

"No, Ronald," Terry said, "never think such a thought. This is Mr. Tucman, a close friend of mine. I called him. He came all the way from Manhattan to help me take care of these painful matters."

"Any of the neighbors would help, Dad," Terry, Jr. said.

"You know I've never felt close to our neighbors. I prefer a close friend."

Trying to explain my presence was hard on Terry. I knew

he wanted me to hold him in my arms and comfort him, but instead, he had to hold his sons in his arms and comfort them and explain the presence of someone he had loved more than he loved their mother.

There was a definite glare of resentment coming toward me through the tears in Ronald's eyes. A gaze of puzzlement came to me from Terry, Jr. He seemed to sense a strangeness about my presence. If I had been a woman, I believe he would have yelled at me and called me his father's whore. I have never considered myself as being the "obvious type" of gay person, but no one would ever mistake me for a truck driver. Somehow I felt that Terry, Jr. subconsciously made a sexual connection about my presence, a connection he would not yet dare let out of his subconscious. An unnamed feeling, an unexpressed thought, something unknown in its first encounter, but something to linger and grow and form itself into first a suspicion, then a searching for knowledge, even unwanted knowledge, and then a digging for the truth. A truth too profound for him to seek and face and believe in his early youth, a youth where purity was manipulated in the palm of his hand and teased in his phantasies. Yet his purity of youth was coated with a tragic death, a death he could not believe, but had to believe because it was there in the blood-water of their bathtub. How could she do this to herself and how could she do this to him, to his father and his brother? What caused her, what drove her to take her life away from them?

My mind raced and swirled with the expression in his eyes. The holding in of his tears caused a mountain of questions to build up in his heart and soul. Ronald, the younger, had blurted out a question, thereby opening a valve in himself and washed out some of his pain with the shedding of his tears, and he seemed, even though reluctantly, to accept the reason his father gave him for this stranger in their home, even in their bathroom.

But Terry, Jr. did not ask in the spoken word. This replica of my lover did not cleanse anything out of him with his tears, the tears only swarm around in the emerald green of his eyes.

He was too beautiful simply to be somebody's son – he

must soon become somebody's lover.

"I'll do anything I can to help you," I said to Terry and his sons. (How strange I felt speaking to the three of them and in the presence of his wife's nude corpse.)

"Just stick by me," Terry said, and the words came from down under, underneath the pain and underneath the tragedy.

"You know I will." I tried not to let the sound of love be too obvious in the tone of my voice, yet I knew it was there.

Terry, Jr. briefly glanced at me again. The look he gave me was not made of daggers; he had not shot me the glance; yet it had penetrated me in such a way that made me feel he wanted to open me up and read and study and explore my insides.

I trembled. And I cannot explain the trembling. It was not a trembling of fear, nor was it a trembling of lust. It was a trembling within me as if the boy's eyes were shaking my soul and asking me to tell him all about the meaning of life and death, and why was I his father's close friend, and why had he never heard his father mention my name until this night of his mother's death.

"I can't believe. I can't believe. I can't believe Mama is dead." Terry, Jr. was whispering, and burying his grief. He was not letting grief accept tragedy.

The tragedy cried out in the red bubbles to be accepted, but he was rejecting the tragedy. He did not let a tear fall. He could have written a wordless book with those tears he did not drop.

His mind set upon me with unformed thoughts.

But I could read Terry's mind: *accept my sons accept my sons accept my sons; forgive them if they do not understand your presence here – they do not understand death... Do we?*

Our eyes had hundreds of times spoken to each other in a room full of love, only love, but now we had to let our eyes communicate in the presence of death. Each knowing that if we had not loved each other, she would not be dead.

But we loved.

Our love demanded its own existence. Our love had birthed itself in passion after a literary cocktail party over eleven years ago and our love had lived on love for all those eleven years.

She had him for six days and six nights all through those years and for seven years before he met me.

I had him for only nine hours a week.

Must the laws of marriage be so selfish?

As these thoughts and questions burned through my blood, I knew I was trying to justify our love in the face of her death, and I could feel these same feelings burning through my lover's heart and blood.

We had a right to love!

We were born to be ourselves.

I had not intended to take all his desire away from her, nor had he intended to let it fade.

And I knew he would have given anything not to have let that outburst of wrath fall upon the mother of his children.

But the burying of dead desire was a long and tedious task, and the corpse of the desire sprang up and cried out against the living of someone he no longer desired.

We heard the doorbell ring.

It was a rude intrusion upon the grief and the tragedy.

"I'll let them in," I said, and left Terry and his sons with the corpse.

A doctor came with the police.

My lover's wife would have to be pronounced dead. The corpse itself was not enough. Some sort of paper, called a death certificate, had to confirm the dead as being dead.

I introduced myself as a friend of Mr. Lane's.

I went with the police and the doctor up the stairs to the bathroom. Terry sent his sons to their bedroom upon the arrival of the police. They asked their questions quietly and respectfully. Terry turned his head away as the doctor reached under the red bubbles and lifted her hand and looked at her slit wrist.

A policeman asked: "Do you have any idea why she did it?"

Terry and I had not had the chance to make up any kind of story, so he told a rearranged truth. He did not tell them the whole truth. He kept to himself the truth of our love.

"For the past few years we have been drifting apart. We never had any serious arguments, hardly any disagreements.

We knew there was a distance growing between us, but we kept a certain respect for each other. We were talking quietly before we went to sleep. She said, 'You love me because I am Terry, Jr. and Ronald's mother. That's the only reason. You no longer love me for myself. You no longer love me, you no longer love me.' She said these words several times. She had accused me before, more than once, of no longer loving her and in the past I had tried to reassure her that the love had simply changed. It usually does with people after eighteen years of marriage. But last night I was simply silent." He paused, knowing this was a lie. Then to assuage the lie, he said: 'Silent about the change of love. Maybe if I had lied to her and told her I loved her as much as ever, she would not have killed herself. I don't know why I didn't. I had had a hard Monday at the office. I was too tired. I, well maybe, I wanted her to accept the truth that, yes, I loved her as the mother of our children, but the love of our youth had changed. Eighteen years can do that to a feeling. We do not usually feel the same at thirty-eight as we do at twenty."

One of the other officers asked, "Is there another woman, Mr. Lane?"

"No," Terry said. "Absolutely not."

Of course the officer did not ask: Is there another man you love? Is the man standing here beside you your lover? Did this man take your love away from your wife?

The officers did not probe the question any deeper. Perhaps they, too, had been married long enough to wander astray.

The doctor asked a question: "At what time did she do it?"

"I'm not sure," Terry said, "not exactly sure. I was asleep and I just happened to wake up and had a strange feeling that something was wrong. My wife was not beside me. That was not unusual. She sometimes got up in the middle of the night and went to the bathroom. Sometimes I awoke, sometimes I didn't. I could not fall asleep again. There was simply that weird feeling that something was wrong. I went to the bathroom and saw what had happened. I was in a daze. I could not believe it. I had to telephone my friend here to come and actually confirm what I saw with my own eyes." (This also was not exactly the truth. I believe his eyes did believe it. It was his heart that could not believe what had happened.) "I didn't even think about calling the police until my friend came and did it for me. She must have gone into the bathroom about two in the morning."

"And you didn't call the police until three-fifty this morning?"

"I couldn't. I was stunned. I had enough of my senses to call someone to help me. I couldn't call the police. It seemed, if I even thought about it, I don't remember, it seemed too cold. Do you understand? I knew instantly, at first glance, she was dead. So I did not call a doctor."

"Just a matter of routine," one of the officers said.

"He was just too shaken up to deal with the routine matters," I said.

Then one of the officers, the one who had been doing most of the talking, looked me in the eye. I cannot swear to it but I think I saw a sense of recognition. I believe he was gay; I believe he knew I was gay.

"Nice to have a friend to take care of such matters for you," he said calmly.

There were a few more questions, but they did not touch upon the relationship of Terry and I. There was the matter of calling the funeral home. I took care of the details for Terry so that I might spare him some of the pain.

When they came to take her away, neither Terry nor I looked at the removal of his wife from the red bubble bath.

We stopped outside the bathroom. The boys glanced outside their bedroom door when they heard something new happening. Terry told them not to look.

"Please don't go," Terry said to me, and he went to his sons, into their room, and stayed with them until the woman who lost her husband to me had been taken away. I don't know who it was that had pulled the plug in the bathtub. From where I was just outside the bathroom, I heard the draining of the water, and as it drained out, it was as if the breath of something was being drained away, not the breath of someone – that had already happened – but the breath of something.

After they had taken the body away, I went into the bathroom and did my best to scrub away the blood stains in the tub. I did not want Terry or his sons to see the remaining signs of suicide.

Now there was a silence of empty death in the house, different from the silence of death while the body was still there.

It was now about five o'clock in the mornng. The night was going away; the sun would soon be up. I wanted to go outside; I wanted to breathe the living dawn as it arose, but I did not want to leave Terry.

I always keep a pen and small note pad in one of my pockets. So I wrote a note to Terry and slipped it under the door of the bedroom. The note said: "Stay with your sons until they are a bit calmer. I'll be on the front porch."

I went outside and I sat in the front porch swing, partially hidden by the ivy, but I could see out clearly. The dawn was coming. The few stars that had been in the sky had gone away. The slender moon hung on.

I knew that Terry would come to me as soon as he could.

There was an emptiness in the pit of my stomach, but I was not hungry. The emptiness was longing for the life of this house. I resented her suicide. How could she do such a horrible thing to her husband and to his sons? After eighteen years of marriage wasn't respect enough? Did she have to have his physical love too? Did she think he had hated her all the years he had loved me? I know he did not hate anyone. Terry Lane could love for a long time, but he could not hate for long. Only momentarily did he despise her, and only some part of her, when she had reached for him earlier this morning.

I knew his body so well it was a part of my senses; her reaching for him was almost as if she had been reaching for me. It was my body, crying out through his voice: "Bitch! Bitch! Don't ever touch me again."

I had never had sex with a woman in all my life. Terry's voice had echoed our bodies.

Sitting there in his front porch swing, just before dawn, I became aware that Terry had not wept. He had sobbed inside himself; like Terry, Jr. he had not shed any cleansing tears, tears to cleanse away the sharp edges of tragedy.

He came onto the front porch.

For a moment he stood still in the doorway.

Then he came to me, and sitting down beside me, he gathered me up into his arms and sank his tongue in my mouth, kissing me with an overflowing abundance of sexual hunger. If any of the neighbors were up and looking our way, they may or may not have been able to see us through the ivy.

I don't think we cared.

"The boys are asleep," he said. "Come to the bedroom. I have to have you. I've never had you in my bed."

"My bed is your bed."

"I know. But I have to have you in my bed upstairs. I have to love some life into it. She threw a cloud of death over me. She should not have done that to the boys and me. Let me suck the life of you into my soul. Let me suck out the feeling of her death. Cover my face with your ass. Fill my throat with your cock. Line my insides with the life of your body-juice. I'm hungry for you, Phillip. I am so hungry for you my insides will burst open if I don't have you to hold me together."

I held him close in my arms; I took his tongue into my mouth and sucked his tongue, wanting to suck away his words of grief.

I reached my hand down between his legs.

He was limp.

"I only want you," he said.

We went up the stairs and into the bedroom that was his and his wife's. We stripped naked. My cock stood high for him but he was still limp.

We were standing beside the bed.

My eyes questioned him.

"Don't let it matter," he said. "I'm beat that way. I'm not feeling passionate in my loins. I am simply so hungry for you I feel as if I am starved for life."

He sat down on the side of the bed in front of me and filled his mouth and his throat with the life-throbbing meat of me. I caressed the hairs of his head and told him of my love for him; he caressed my buttocks and the hairs around my asshole as he devoured me.

He had never before gone about it so desperately. Two or three times I felt his teeth, but I did not mention the slight pain. I knew his desperation must be soothed; I knew my staff of life was the only thing in life that could caress and ease the hardness of his grief in the face of death.

His passionate hunger mounted with the mounting of my physical passion; he knew the quickening of my flesh just before the coming of my cream, and his fingers sank between my buttocks. And as I poured my life-giving juices into him, he swallowed as if he wanted to swallow my entire being, as if he wanted to drain me inside himself, underneath his skin and make us truly as one, for we had been spiritually united years ago, and now the flesh wanted to become as the spirit.

After I emptied myself into him, he still clung to life's passion, and I did not immediately go limp – it stayed up for a considerable time and I knew he needed the quiet upness of it so that it might continue to soothe his desperation. Then slowly, slowly, I became limp and his tongue caressed the limpness.

Then he let it fall from between his lips and he pressed his face into my pubic hair. "Phillip. Phillip. You are my life."

He licked my belly, still caressing the hairs between my buttocks. He drew his feet upon the bed. He was slowly lying down and drawing me down to the bed, and from times experienced, many times with him, I knew what he wanted. He adjusted the pillows under his head – his pillow and his deceased wife's pillow – and I turned as I crawled onto the bed and sat down on his face; and the passionate hunger of his mouth clamped upon my ass as his tongue probed my asshole, trying to wedge an entrance into me. I clenched and unclenched my buttocks, grasping and releasing his tongue, and praying to God, there on my knees, praying to God that he would, that he could, suck out the pain of this tragedy.

His hunger was intense. His hunger was powerful. Surely his grief would be soothed.

I felt as if he were trying to draw my spine out of me and swallow my spine and make it an internal part of himself.

I caressed his chest and his belly while he ate my ass. There were times when a rippling quiver ran through his body, and I prayed again and again to God to cleanse my love of his buried grief and cleanse him of any guilt that he might harbor inside his beautiful being.

I leaned over, my buttocks still upon his beautiful face, and I took his limpness into my mouth and I worked upon it. But he remained limp. There was a hardness of stone in his soul, a soul filled with buried tears, solidified tears, tears turned to stone because he could not bring them out in the open and air them, and the hard buried tears took the place of the hardness of his meat. He could not let his soul go limp with grief and weep away drops of pain.

She had killed his staff of life when she killed herself.

I tried to bring it back to life. I worked upon the resurrection of his lifeline.

But he was limp.

I tried another way. I placed his legs behind my arms, my hands under his buttocks and drew his ass up to my mouth and I soul-kissed his asshole as he was doing the same to me, praying to God that I could melt the stone in his soul with this intimate soul-kiss that I considered to be the ultimate in intimacy.

I wanted to suck the grief out of him as I had heard of people sucking poison out of a person who has been bitten by a snake, for I knew the poison of unreleased grief can be a slow draining away of the living life of a human being, leaving only a living death.

My mouth worked in ecstasy and anxiety there between the buttocks of my beloved, trying desperately to draw from the nerves of his spinal cord the hardened nerves of grief.

We sucked on beyond the dawn.

The morning sun came in but his heart was still in the darkness of himself.

He imprisoned the image of a corpse somewhere in the cell of his soul.

She took a part of my lover to the morgue with her, and she would take a part of him to the grave.

She had not intended to be vicious. She simply, as a mother and a wife, took with her into her bath the vital organs of her husband, and the bubbles became the ghost of their faded love. She acted quietly. In the slitting of her wrists, she severed certain vessels within his loins, and she

118

left him as limp as their lost love.

Perhaps she had not intended to attack him and wound him, but the ghost of her stabbed him below the waist.

Call it his own buried guilt, if you must, but she performed the act that caused the guilt.

She did the killing, he did the burying.

His once-hard cock changed into a shovel and the shovel buried the passion of his loins in the skin of limp dreams.

His cock could no longer stand up for itself and proclaim its right to be loved.

The passion that had once glowed beautifully in his loins raged into his mouth and he became ravenously hungry.

My jaws tired long before his jaws and I tried to free myself from his grasping embrace, but he did not want to let go of my ass. "No, not yet," he pleaded. "Please, please, let me suck and suck and suck."

The sun brought the light into the bedroom but the darkness stayed in his heart.

Chapter 12

I LOST MY love.

No. I never lost my love for Terry Lane. Even after all these years, I still love that beautiful man.

I lost the body of my lover.

And even that is not exactly true. She took him away from me and threw him to the wolves.

She had been, from what I had heard him tell me about her, a quiet and gracious lady up until the time of her death. And then the ghost of her became vicious.

Time and time again I talked with him and tried to persuade him that he was not to blame for her death. Intellectually he believed me, but emotionally he was trapped in her grave by the shock she had given to his emotions. Her ghost clawed at his cock and balls, and she drew them down into the grave with her, and his staff of life never rose again.

Her death rankled in his spirit. Her death changed him.

That morning after her death, he did not free my ass from his mouth until we heard his sons up and about.

He let go of me, and he became the father of his sons.

As I dressed, he put on his robe, I remember the yellow and green pattern of the robe – there was a green dragon embroidered on the back of the robe, red fires came from the dragon's nostrils; its claws were set for attack, the background was yellow. His wife had graciously given it to him for his thirty- seventh birthday.

He stepped outside the bedroom, closing the door behind him.

I heard him speaking to his sons: "We'll have to prepare our own breakfast now, fellows. We'll have to learn to get along without your mother. It won't be easy. But remember, I love you. Try to forgive her for leaving us." There was a pause. "My friend stayed with me last night. It was too late, too early in the morning for him to make the trip back to Manhattan."

The boys did not ask why it was too late. The boys did not ask why I was sleeping in their deceased mother's bed instead of sleeping on the living room couch that let out into a bed. They did not ask questions, they tucked them away inside themselves, or cast them aside. I believe that Ronald was able to cast anything aside, as able as he was at shedding tears. I believe that Terry, Jr. tucked a number of questions inside his heart and let them move around inside him.

"We'll be downstairs in a few minutes," Terry said. "I'll cook our breakfast."

He came back into the bedroom with me. He walked directly over and took my crotch in his hand. I had my trousers and shoes on. "Let me do it again," he said.

"I came twice, Terry. Maybe we had better see about breakfast with your sons."

"I'm still hungry for you, Phillip. You're my breakfast, my lunch, my dinner."

"I love you, Terry. I love you. Let's take it easy." I was drained. My ass felt raw. Nevertheless, if it had not been for his sons, waiting for us downstairs, I would have gone to bed with him again.

I had not showered. He did not shower. We usually did not shower as we parted. We wanted to keep the feeling and the aroma of each other on our flesh.

He slipped into his shorts, saying, "Forgive me for being limp."

"You know you never have to apologize to me."

"Maybe I'm apologizing to my prick."

He put on his trousers and a sports shirt, his socks and shoes.

I felt awkward, having breakfast with my lover and his sons. I felt their awkwardness. Very little was said. Now and then I could feel Terry, Jr's. gaze upon me. He might have been a surgeon, examining me for some defective organ to be removed, but not quite sure what the organ was or where it was located or if it was really defective.

While I was in their deceased mother's bed with their father, I did not feel in the least like an intruder, but here at the breakfast table with the two boys, I felt like an unwanted stranger on strange territory.

I believe this was the first and only time that Terry Lane and I had ever had breakfast together.

The ghost of his wife was hovering over us and between us. Yet I knew that Terry was not hungry for his bacon and eggs. I knew he was still hungry for cock and ass.

There was too much silence.

Occasionally Terry, Jr's. emerald eyes, astonishingly like his father's, swept over me and away from me. His eyes did not undress me as gay eyes have a way of doing. They stripped my flesh from my bones and questioned the marrow of my bones. He said hardly a word. I couldn't help but wonder if he had ever been approached by man or woman. His beauty could do as much toward frightening others away as it could toward drawing others to him. His beauty could be his friend. His beauty could be his enemy.

His eggs were scrambled. Ronald's eggs were sunny side up. Terry, Jr. took cream in his coffee. Ronald took his black. Terry, Jr. had carefully combed his hair before breakfast. Ronald had given his a lick and a promise. Were they virgins? Had they been had? Did they frequently engage in mutual masturbation? How far did they take their experimentations?

Was I being subconsciously, subcutaneously, unfaithful to Terry?

I tried to get my mind off my lover's sons.

My heart wept for Terry.

I had not seen a single tear in his eyes. I had heard him sob hard and painful sobs, but there had been no soft tears. I had seen tears swimming around in Terry, Jr's. eyes, but I had not seen them fall. Ronald was the only one of the three who opened up and released his grief in the form of cleansing tears.

I do not believe that Terry had sucked out his grief; I believe he had sucked out some of the pain that sat on top of the grief, but, no, not the grief itself.

"You won't go to work today, will you, Dad?" Ronald

122

asked.

"No. I'll take the week off. It's not nine o'clock yet. I'll call at nine and let them know."

"I can't believe she's gone," Terry, Jr. said.

"She's dead," Terry said. He did not say she's gone.

"Do people ever understand things like this, Dad?" Ronald asked.

Terry paused. Then he said pensively, "I'm not sure we ever completely understand anything."

"Life and death are deeper than our powers of comprehension," I commented. "Some things we have to accept without knowing why."

"Why?" Terry, Jr. asked. "Why do we have to accept without knowing why we accept?"

"Otherwise, such as in times like this, the pain becomes too much to bear."

"No matter what, she should not have done it to us," Terry, Jr. said, and there was a trace of resentment in his tone of voice.

"I agree with you," Terry said. "But let's try not to judge her. Let's try to forgive her."

"Maybe she had cancer," Ronald said, "and maybe she didn't want anybody else to know and maybe she didn't want to suffer a long time like people do who have cancer."

No, your father's love for me is not a cancer, I wanted to say. But I held my peace. Terry was silent but he was not at peace. I could not expect him to be. His wife's death had caused a sudden change in him. In some ways, he was the same man, but in other ways, I could almost feel a further change taking place as we sat at the breakfast table, and this became more apparent as time went along. There was a repressed agitation stirring around inside him. Even though he had told his sons "we must forgive her," I felt as if he wanted to go to the funeral parlor and curse her for having brought this tragedy down upon him and his sons. Yet there was a thread of feeling, a very slender thread, that some part of him was pleased she would no longer be in his bed.

Until I came, no one else had ever been in that bed except him and his wife.

We were not wrong in having sex there – he had to have

the life of me to replace the death of her.

Was he free now to be all mine?

No. I knew he wasn't. A very basic part of him belonged to his sons. I could not move in and take the place of their mother. I had no maternal feelings. In any event, could I have been comfortable living in the home of my lover with his two teenage sons, two beautiful boys? I don't know. Ronald would not have bothered me, but I suspect that Terry, Jr., being a sixteen year old version of his father, might have upset my bloodstream. However, the question never came up at the time. It was only afterwards that I questioned myself, wondering if that might have helped Terry Lane if I had lived with him day and night, night after night, day by day.

My lover changed.

He never stopped loving me as long as he lived. No matter what, I shall never believe that Terry ever stopped loving me.

Time soon revealed his inability to deal with his wife's self-inflicted violet death. The act of a thin razor in a bubble bath drew him down, pulled him down and crushed parts of him. His integrity crumbled. He stepped on his self-respect. He lost interest in his work, and yet he worked too hard; he threw a driving, resentful force into his work. His intensity increased, becoming a high-pitched nervous intensity. He began to drink heavily and he became a chain smoker. He did not take to drugs – drugs were not fashionable in those days. People had other ways of self-destruction.

These things pained me as I saw them happening in him, but what pained me the most was the fact that he went wild, sexually wild, a madness set upon his tongue and would not let him rest.

The wildness began that morning of her death, the morning when he sucked me beyond the dawn and was still ravenously hungry for me.

After his wife's burial, he came to me for an hour or two every evening before going home to his sons. He sucked me to a point beyond pleasure. Each time I had to almost make him stop.

"Good God, Terry, let me rest."

"Don't make me stop."

"But I've come, Terry. Let me rest."

"Then just let me suck your asshole. I don't want to stop sucking."

And it was hard for him to stop, but his organ never became hard again.

And he was hard on himself about this, each time begging me to forgive him, because he knew that ordinarily my oral desires were as strong as his. Now it was not so much that his oral desires were strong, they were insatiable. He wanted to drown his grief and his guilt in the coming of cream from my staff of life.

But after a time, how long I don't remember, a few weeks, a few months, it became not only my cream for drowning, it became not only my staff of life.

He told me how the first time happened, the first time he was unfaithful to me. And he begged for my forgiveness.

Terry had been working overtime, and one of his ambitious assistants worked with him. Two of the women in the office were also working that evening, but not any of the other men had stayed. Terry had ordered sandwiches and coffee to be sent up to them, and after eating, Terry went to the men's room to wash up and take a leak. He washed his hands first because he did not want to get mayonnaise on his penis. Then while he was standing at the urinal, taking a long, healthy leak, his assistant came in. Terry said he felt his assistant's eyes on his penis as he walked over to the urinal and took out his penis as if to take a leak. But he didn't do anything. He just stood there. When Terry finished he took his time about shaking off that last drop. The assistant had not done anything. He was simply standing there with a nice size penis hanging out.

"Without even thinking about it, with no thoughts coming into my head, I didn't ask, I simply leaned over and went down on him. He didn't make a sound. It was quick. Apparently, he had been in need of it. After he came, I straightened up and said, 'Time to get back to work.'"

"Yes, sir, I'll be right there."

"Nothing was said about it while we worked. I did not bother to look in his eyes to see what he was thinking. And I don't think he had the courage to look me in the eye to see what I was thinking. An hour or so later, we decided we had had it for the night. I have a habit of going to the men's room before I leave work. I don't know if I had to go or not, I simply went. My assistant followed. This time he pissed. While he was shaking off the last drops, I saw it was beginning to grow in size, so I leaned over and took it. After he came, I couldn't let go; I wouldn't let go. The girls had gone on ahead of us. We were alone. I kept doing him. He begged me to let him rest awhile first. He said he was too sensitive afterwards. But I grabbed hold of his buttocks and kept on at it until he came again. And then I came to you and did you. I've gone mad, Phillip. I've gone cock-mad. And I can't get my own cock up. Maybe that's a part of the reason for my madness. My mouth is trying to make up for what my cock can't do, replacing the inabilities of my own cock with the cock of others. Phillip, try to forgive me. Try to understand my madness. The real me wants no one but you, but when my wife killed herself, she struck off a spark of madness in me, and all I want to do is suck suck suck. I no longer know how to talk to my sons. They asked me the other day why I am always so keyed up. 'Ever since Mama died you've been keyed up.' 'Try to forgive me,' I said. 'Maybe I'll calm down after a while. I need to forget what happened.'"

But he did not forget. The reddish-pink water in the tub that night grew blushingly red in his mind. He did not calm down.

As the weeks and the months passed, the dignified man who had been my lover threw away his dignity and became extremely promiscuous. His ravenous technique became almost painful. There was a wildness in his mouth that would not be quiet, that could not be satisfied.

"That's all I think about," he said. "I'm working longer hours and doing less work and I'm drinking too much. I've gone down on every man in the office at least once. There are twenty-five guys working in my department. Only two of them put up any resistance, and their resistance wasn't hard to break down. Still you are the one I love, Phillip. You are the only one I love."

But the purity and the beauty had gone out of our love. Not the memory of it. A thousand men could not take away the memory of our beautiful eleven years of love. How I had respected his integrity! I had admired his regularity. He was a man of honor. Oh, I know there are many who would say that a man who "cheats" on his wife is not a man of honor. I simply say that he did it in an honorable way, and was it really "cheating" when he had told her before their marriage that he was bisexual? I think not. I never knew a more gracious, dignified, honorable man than Terry Lane was before his wife killed herself and killed a part of him. In many ways, he had truly loved her. The physical way had faded. The thing, whatever it is, that holds a man together began to fall apart.

He did not always go home to his sons. In a drunken state he would say, "They're almost grown. They can take care of themselves. Lemme do you just one more time, Phillip. If you're too tired just lemme rim you, rim you, and then you know what... lemme rim you some more." My ass was constantly raw.

The beauty of his love faded away and became a desperate love. I knew he still loved me, thank God, I knew that. I could see the pleading in his emerald eyes, pleading for more of me, pleading in his eyes and with his voice to forgive him for "fooling around" with all those others.

"They mean nothing to me," he said. "At least, they mean nothing to my heart and soul. It's just this wild thing in my mouth, and something swirling around in my mind that I'm trying to satisfy, trying to calm down. But it won't stay calm. There is something like a noise in my head, the noise of lust, that's what it is, and it won't leave me alone. I want it to be again with us the way it was for those eleven years of bliss. This is not bliss I'm having now with those others. It's hot, but it's hot as hell, just as if the fires of hell are burning in my blood and my mouth and my mind. Oh, God, Phillip, forgive me, forgive me, in my heart there is no one but you, forgive me, forgive me. Be patient with me."

I forgave him. Again and again. I was patient with him, even though my patience sometimes felt as raw as my ass. I could not stop loving him. In many ways he was a different man, but deep inside himself he was still the man I loved.

Several times I suggested to him that he see a psychiatrist, but this stirred up a resistance in him that was not logical. He would not discuss it. I believe it was the only thing we ever really seriously argued about. I did not argue with him about the other men he latched onto, because, for one reason, he unlatched them from his jaws after only a few times at it and generally after the first time. But basically, I forgave him because I believed he was experiencing the illness of guilt after his wife's suicide. Yet, no matter how much I urged him not to feel guilty, there were elements of self-incrimination brewing inside him. They did not diminish in the promiscuity. They were only covered up, momentarily half-hidden from himself.

Numbers of times he beat himself up, remembering: "If only I had not called her a bitch. Bitch. Bitch. Now here I am making a bitch of myself."

"See a psychiatrist, Terry."

"Go to hell!" he yelled.

But then he would clamp his mouth onto my mouth and cry into my mouth, "Don't ever go. Don't ever leave me. Never never take yourself away from me. Don't ever let me go all the way away from you. Forgive, forgive, forgive me."

I always forgave him.

Chapter 13

I DO NOT know for certain if Terry Lane became an alcoholic. As I have previously indicated, I do know he became a cockoholic. His mind was constantly inebriated with oral desire. And it seemed to me he became a cigarette fiend. He was smoking less than a pack a day before his wife slit her wrist; within a few months after her death, he was smoking three packs a day. He came to me two or three times a week, and if he wasn't drunk he was high.

One way or another, he wanted a constant flame in his mouth.

I did not love this new person; I did not love these new things abut him, yet underneath, somewhere, there was still the man I loved.

Since he was fooling around with so many others, there came a time when I tried doing it with another man. Terry saw to it that my genitals were more than satisfied, but rimming him and kissing him and sucking his limp was not enough to satisfy my oral desires.

I picked up a piece of trade.

And that's all he was. It was okay. It was good. It somewhat satisfied a need in this orally oriented person. But he was just a piece of meat with cream. I hardly thought of him as a real human being. He remains a faceless blank in my mind. My memory sees his genitals and nothing else.

I have often thought of trade as being genitals with some sort of motorized facsimile of a male behind them.

For two years after the death of Terry Lane's wife our lives went along in that way – innumerable pieces of trade for Terry, and I would guess there were ten or fifteen blank faces with erections for me. I usually met them in bars. Once going up in the elevator in my apartment building. That one happened to be a drunkened bridegroom who was complaining that he had made a mistake in getting married, he just wanted to get laid. So I soothed the bridegroom's complaint.

However, Terry's wildness, which had begun in the men's room of his office, not only went to the bars, his wildness took him to the baths, and the streets, and the subway men's rooms, the men's rooms of theaters and movies and restaurants. He heard of a glory-hole in the men's room of a cafeteria in the basement of one of New York's most well-known hospitals. He would go there and simply place his mouth to the glory-hole and service unseen strangers.

Yet all these men could not shoot it out of him or wash from him the guilt he felt about his deceased wife.

The excess drinking did not help

The excess smoking did not help.

There came the time, approximately two years after his wife's death, when ten days passed that I did not see Terry Lane.

We had years ago established an agreement that I would not call his office or his home except in case of emergency. Of course discretion had long since been blown to the winds. All the men there knew he was gay and had had at least one sample of his gayness, and some of the women knew what was going on.

So I called his office and asked to speak to him.

"Who's calling, please?"

"A personal friend."

"Have you been a personal friend of Mr. Lane's for long?"

"A very close friend for thirteen years."

"Then I think you should know, and I am very sorry to have to tell you, Mr. Lane suffered a serious stroke seven days ago."

"Oh, my God." I drew in my breath, drawing in the strength to ask, "Is he living?"

"Just barely. The stroke happened here in the office, just after lunch one afternoon. I am afraid he had been drinking heavily. He was sent to the New York Hospital. I can give you the address and telephone number of the hospital if you wish, but if you plan to visit he probably won't recognize you."

"Yes. I would appreciate the address and telephone number."

I wrote down the information the young lady on the telephone gave me. Then I asked, "Do you know anything about his children? They are nearly grown, but I suppose someone needs to take care of matters."

"His sister came up from Florida. She is making arrangements to have him placed in a nursing home. I believe it is called the Sunnyside Nursing Home in Queens. But I have heard he will be at the New York Hospital for another two weeks or so. The doctors say he will never fully recover. I am so sorry to have to tell you these things."

"Thank you. Thank you. You have been very kind."

I hung up.

I hung up on a part of my life.

My heart sank into my belly. I felt tears slowly drifting down my face.

The past two years had not been very romantic. But what hell they had been for Terry, trying to suck his way out of grief, out of guilt. Trying to drink his way out of it. Trying to smoke his way out of hell.

It was not very widely known in those days that cigarette smoking can be bad for a person's circulation. However, a recent acquaintance of mine, who is a specialist in vascular diseases, tells me it is the worst thing a person can do. And of course the circulatory system is directly involved with strokes. Alcoholism or even semi-alcoholism is extremely bad for a person's blood pressure. I did not know Terry Lane had high blood pressure, and I doubt that he knew. The high tension of his compulsive promiscuity added to the causes of the stroke.

My God, he was only forty.

I wept for a while, quietly, silently, meditatively.

I let my memory go back before the last two years, and I felt again the beauty of those previous eleven years of our romance.

But the reality of the day drew me back to the tragedy of Terry Lane.

It was still morning.

I called the hospital and asked if I could visit Terry Lane.

"Are you a relative?"

"No. But I am a close friend. We have been the closest of friends for thirteen years."

Should I tell the person on the phone that my insides were lined with his semen? Should I tell that stranger that the patient's insides were lined with my semen, and forget about the hundreds of others who had cum during the past two years – their semen had passed on out of him – no, their semen had not lined his heart and soul – the internal lining of that beautiful man was the semen of his only real love, myself.

"I suppose it will be all right for you to see him. But he probably won't recognize you."

"Thank you."

Terry Lane not recognize Phillip Tucman? Don't be foolish, lady. Don't be foolish. Terry would recognize me anywhere. No matter what.

But I was mistaken.

I went to my beloved in the hospital immediately after lunch. A nurse showed me to his room. A gay attendant passed me carrying a bed pan.

Terry was in a private room.

I went in and closed the door behind me.

"Terry," I spoke with a smile.

"What are you doing here? How are you, man? Terry. Terry." My tone fell. I whispered: "Terry. Terry."

His eyes were open. But they were not his eyes. The emeralds had lost their glow. One side of his face was drawn down and distorted. His lips, lips I had known thousands of times; his lips, lips that had given me the greatest intimacy one man can give another – his lips were twisted.

I went to him and I kissed those twisted lips. I kissed his semi-dead eyes.

"I love you, Terry. I love you."

He was being fed intravenously.

I took one of his hands in mine. He did not respond.

How could he be this way? How could life do this terrible thing to such a beautiful man? Why must life take something beautiful and change it into something ugly? That side of his face, his paralyzed side, did not belong to Terry Lane. Some monstrous quirk of life, destiny, fate, had stolen his beauty away from him.

Yet, I could not see him as ugly. What had happened to him tore my heart out and cast a veil, the veil of a bleeding heart, over him as he lay there, and I saw him in my memory as the most beautiful love of my life.

The dead emeralds took away the glow of his eyes.

Still my tears fell on his distorted cheek and I saw through the veil of tears and I saw through memory, and I saw a very sick man.

Some part of my spirit, some part of my soul, seeped out of me and crawled into bed with my lover and crawled under his pajamas and seeped into the pores of his body, some part of me became Terry, some part of me was Terry, the soul of my love became his one evening after a literary cocktail party, and my soul and I had been his for these thirteen years.

That man who had gone wild was not the Terry Lane I knew; this man here on the bed in a hospital was not the same man.

Time distorted him. Time turned its mirror the wrong way and revealed a stranger living, now dying, in the form of Terry Lane.

Time was a bastard!

I sank to the floor on my knees beside his bed, and I held his unresponsive hand between the palms of my two hands, folded in prayer, and I prayed to God to give him back to me.

But God does not always deem it wise to answer all our prayers.

Who can know the meaning of unanswered prayers?

Perhaps it is best we do not know all we want to know. Was this some sort of punishment God had cast down on Terry Lane for calling his wife a bitch? Was Terry being punished for being wild? Was he being punished, and was I now being punished, for the love we had shared with each other so beautifully during the previous eleven years? – dropping from the sight of the heart the past two years.

No. I cannot believe that God is a cruel God. I do not believe that life is cruel. The events that happen are sometimes cruel. Time is not always a bastard, time is only sometimes a bastard.

The beauty of a rose does not last forever. No rose was ever more beautiful than the lips of my beloved during those years of our bliss.

I can see and say and write these things now, but during the months that followed Terry Lane's stroke I felt a bitterness in my heart and a swirling of resentments in my mind.

What was the matter with medical science that it could not, now in the nineteen sixties, cure and restore this victim of a stroke? The doctors told me they were doctors, not gods or miracle workers. Medical science was a science, not a miracle. Yet there were some stroke victims who did make amazing progress and almost recover. That, however, depended upon the severity of the damage done to the brain and the nervous system.

Terry Lane's stroke had been extremely severe.

Chapter 14

I WAS STILL seeing Walter and Vera Smothers every Friday during all these years.

When I told them about the suicide of Terry Lane's wife, there was a long silence. It was almost as if the silence was saying: What else could the poor woman do? You took her husband's love away from her. How does that make you feel?

But to cover up the sound of the questions in the silence, Walter said, "Of course it was no fault of yours."

"It's shocking," Vera said. "Such things are always shocking. But when a person kills herself or himself, how can it be anyone else's fault but their own?"

"She knew what was going on all those years, seems like she might have realized he would eventually stop wanting her," Walter said, and his eyes seemed to cut into me, trying to cut out a slice of my feelings and examine me too excruciatingly close.

"I don't think I feel any guilt about it," I said. "But sometimes I hate her for doing this to Terry."

"And the boys, of course," Vera said.

"Of course," I agreed.

"I don't think people have the right to commit suicide unless they have a terminal illness," Vera said.

"There is no way to determine the rights and the wrongs of a suicide," Walter said emphatically. "If a person wants to die, should he or she be forced to live?"

"Oh, Walter," Vera said. "That question makes me shudder."

Two years and three weeks later, Vera called me and told me that Walter had killed himself. He killed himself in the same way that Terry's wife had killed herself, by slitting his wrist in a tub of hot water, only he did not bother with the bubbles.

Several days after I had told Walter and Vera about Terry's near-fatal stroke, Walter called me from a bar near Times Square on Forty-forth Street, East of Broadway. It was a gay bar. It was two o'clock in the morning. He was drunk. His words slurred.

"I've got to talk to you," he demanded. "Come have a drink with me. I'm in Arty's Bar."

"Good God, Walter. Get yourself together and go home."

"What is home? What is all this flag-waving shit everybody preaches about home? Home Sweet Shit Shit Shit. It's too goddamn sweet." He began to cry into the telephone. "Come talk to me," he begged. "Talk to me. That's the goddamned least you can do."

"Take it easy, Walter. I'll be there as soon as I can get there. Don't have anymore to drink."

"I'll drink all I goddamned want to drink." He slung the receiver down on the hook.

I suspected what Walter would want to talk about; the bubbles around his mouth would transform themselves into the expostulations of truth.

Poor Walter.

If there was ever a man to admire and hold in contempt simultaneously, it was Walter. Such a brilliant mind! And so full of shit! Now it was time for the shit to hit the fan, and I had been chosen as the fan. Somehow I always believed it would happen, but it happened in a way even more profound than I had expected.

When I went into the barroom the Juke Box was lamenting about "The Man Who Got Away." There was an uneven hum of voices, punctured by an occasional squeal. There was an odor of beer and smoke. Everyone looked on the verge.

Walter was waiting for me near the entrance.

"There you are. You're here," he said, and grabbed me by the lapels of my jacket. "I got to tell you."

"Easy, Walter. Easy."

"It's never been easy. It's been hell. Fucking hell. Let's sit in that booth over there. Alone."

He was shoving me toward the booth. I almost fell onto the seat. He did not sit across from me. He sat beside me, shoving me against the wall, his leg pressing against my leg.

"I got to tell you," he blurted. He was so drunk, it was amazing he could even speak. His eyes were swimming in tears and fear and passion. The intellectual facade had fallen beneath the booze.

"I love you," he said. "You goddamn bastard, you never thought about me loving you. I love you so much I could eat you, and I want to eat you. Now that guy's dying – you know he's dying, don't you? – you gotta have a place in your life for me. Friday night friendship! I eat my heart out every time I see you. I want us to do everything you and that guy did. Damn it damn it damn it! I can love you just as much as he ever loved you. I'm hot and hungry."

"And drunk," I added. "You don't know what you are saying, Walter. You don't mean it."

"That's a lie. You know fucking well I know what I'm' saying. I've been saying it inside myself for years, and I know you know I want you."

He grabbed at my crotch and hurt my balls.

"Stop it. That hurt."

"I'm hurting inside myself. Love me, Phillip. Love me, love me."

"I love you as a friend, Walter."

"No. We had enough of that. Love me, love me as a lover loves a lover. I want to eat you. I'm so hungry, I'm dying."

"You won't die, Walter."

"How th' hell do you know? You've been carrying on with that guy all these years, and never thought of me the way I thought and thought and thought of you. I don't blame his wife, I goddamned well don't blame her."

"Easy, Walter." (How many times did I say that? There wasn't much else I could say. I simply tried.) "I'm your friend, Walter. A close friend to you and Vera. The three of us are very close friends, Walter. And friendship is a good thing to maintain."

"Maintain my ass! How many times you think I do it with my wife and pretend it's your lips or your little snob ass?"

"Believe me, my ass is not a snob."

"You snob my prick. You snob my love. I got to, I just got to have you."

"It can't be that way, Walter."

"Why th' goddamn hell not? You think my throat ain't deep enough? I can take every goddamn inch you got. You want my tongue up your ass? Gimme your ass, I'll stick it up there. Lean over this goddamn table. Lean over. You think I care who knows? I been hiding myself from my wife all these goddamn years. My wife sees only what she wants to see."

"You don't mean what you're saying, Walter." (I knew he did mean it.) "We don't want Vera to know about this."

"That's right, we don't want Vera to know. Vera's my wife. I'm Vera's husband. You be my husband. Ram your prick up my ass and be my husband. Shove some wedding bells down my throat, but who wants wedding bells? Balls are better'n bells."

He grabbed at my balls.

"Stop it, Walter. Stop it."

"I gotta stop before I start. That's th' goddamn blank history of my gay sex life. Phillip, Phillip, I'm so drunk. I think I'll sleep here on this pretty ugly table. Look, somebody carved a mouth and a prick. Phillip, I'm sleepy." He slumped over. His slobbery mouth fell upon the carving.

The Juke Box was playing "That Old Black Magic".

I had noticed a muscular young hustler leaning against the Juke Box, grinning in our direction, while he nursed the beer he couldn't afford, waiting for someone who would pay for his beer or his body.

I motioned for him to come over to our booth.

He strolled over, crotch first.

"Hi ya," he said. "Your friend pass out? I don't pass out. I never passed out in all my life."

He was about twenty-two, so that left him plenty of time to get around to passing out.

"I'll give you five bucks to help me get him into a cab."

"Sure. Be happy to oblige. I get ten for the night. I've been told I'm great."

"I'll bet you're more than great. But all I want you to do is help me carry him out and hold him up while I get a cab."

"Yeah, sure. But I just thought I'd let you know I'm

available."

Every fibre of his body was letting everybody know he was available.

He began to lift Walter up. I slid out of the booth and attempted to give a hand, but the young stud was doing okay. However, when I saw the young stud's hand ooze down toward Walter's hip where his wallet was halfway sticking out, I took the wallet and said, "We don't want to lose this, do we."

"Oh, no, of course not."

Outside the barroom door the nameless stud held up Walter while I hailed a cab. Then as we maneuvered Walter into the cab, the hustler said, "Only ten bucks for the whole night."

"Maybe some other time," I said, sitting Walter on the far side of the seat. "Here's five. Good luck."

"I've been told I'm wonderful."

"I'll bet you have."

The driver drove away.

I knew the muscular stud would not starve.

When we arrived at Walter and Vera's apartment house, I promised the driver a big tip if he would help me get Walter into the building. He was a nice guy. He gave me a hand with Walter, not only into the building but into the elevator and to his apartment on the third floor. He waited with me while I rang the bell and Vera came to the door.

"Oh, my Lord in Heaven," she said. "Oh, my Lord, my Lord, my Lord."

She was halfway praying and halfway referring to Walter as her Lord and Master.

I thanked the driver and paid him.

Vera held Walter up under his armpit on one side, and we managed to get him inside and into the bedroom where he slumped down onto the bed.

"I'm so grateful to you, Phillip," Vera said as she began undressing him for bed. "You haven't been drinking, I can tell. So who was he drinking with? What happened? I'm not sure I want to know. So don't tell me anything if you don't want to."

"The telephone woke me at two o'clock. He was calling

from a bar in Times Square, and asked me to come and get him. He was too drunk to make it home alone."

"He doesn't seem to be himself recently. Strange, so strange. He started drinking heavily the day after you told us about your friend's stroke. He's been drinking much too much during the past couple of weeks, Phillip. I don't understand. But there is so much I don't understand. I worship my husband. But sometimes I think I am married to half a stranger. Some part of Walter has never introduced himself to me."

"There isn't a human being in the world who doesn't have a dark side to his nature, Vera."

"I know. I suppose I know. If you'll help me put his feet on the bed, I'll let him sleep it off."

"Of course."

"Have a cup of hot chocolate with me, Phillip. I need to talk to somebody. You are our closest friend."

"Of course, Vera."

Our talk rambled on until dawn. I had the feeling that Vera wanted to get at something, and yet she talked in circles, because some part of her did not want to acknowledge some part of her husband. She wanted to live in a marriage of illusion, but recently Walter's heavy drinking was washing away the illusion.

She said such things as: "When he makes love to me recently, he's being almost vicious."

"But not actually vicious."

"No. But sometimes I wonder if he thinks I am somebody else. Yet I know he isn't having any kind of an affair. I believe a wife usually knows."

"I doubt very much he's having an affair, Vera."

"He doesn't love me all the way. I don't believe he has ever loved me as much as I love him. I love him as I know him and I love the stranger inside the darkness of him." She paused. "But I'm afraid of that stranger. Sometimes I'm afraid that stranger will take Walter away from me."

"I don't think anyone could actually take Walter away from you, Vera."

"I wouldn't be myself without Walter."

Now and then she looked at me as if to say: You know

something I need to know but don't want to know. Tell me, but don't let me hear you. Tell me, but don't let me believe you.

I did not tell her the bar was gay. I did not tell her my friend, her husband, attempted to seduce me. I could not tell Vera these things.

Vera was one of those people you simply want to naturally protect.

"What shall I do, Phillip?"

"Let him sleep it off."

"And when he gets drunk again?"

"Maybe he won't."

"He will. I know he will. I wish I knew why, but maybe I don't want to know why, why he started drinking so much right after you told him about your friend having a stroke. Do you think Walter is afraid he is going to have a stroke?"

"That may have something to do with it. Seems to me I've read somewhere that when a man reaches forty he needs to start taking a little better care of himself."

"That's only natural."

"Wait it out, Vera. Give him a chance to get over whatever it is that's bothering him."

"I think whatever it is has been bothering him all his life, but it simply reached a peak recently. Sometimes I think he is going to explode, not in anger, but explode with whatever he has been holding down inside himself. If he explodes, he'll fall apart. Walter can't face some things. Like years ago, I believe you may remember, we tried and tried to have a baby. I was thoroughly examined, and found to be fertile. The doctor wanted Walter to be examined, but he refused. He refused to face the possibility that his seed might not be strong enough to reach the egg. So we have no children."

I could not tell her that Walter was now facing his homosexuality, or his bisexuality, but not facing up to it very well. Then I asked myself what would Walter have done if I had bought the male hustler for him, taken them to my place, let them alone, and let them carry on for an hour or so? Would that have been a good idea? Would that have released something inside Walter that needed releasing? Or would it have simply opened the lid on a steaming sexual spiral and helped him to come out and go as wild as Terry Lane had gone? Or was it, as Walter had implied, only me that he wanted?

"Sometimes I think I almost know," Vera was saying, "what it is that's bothering Walter. But just as he can't face certain things, there are things maybe I can't face. That stranger inside him. Maybe I need to know that stranger. But I don't want to know that stranger."

"Do we have to know everything, Vera?"

"I don't know."

"Sometimes a little mystery between people maybe helps to keep the relationship going, adds a touch of on-going excitement to it."

"Or stabs it in the dark," Vera said, for a second or two drifting off into a trance.

"What do you mean by that?"?

"I don't know. But I think you are right, I'm afraid if I knew everything I would go mad. I would lose my mind in a pile of human knowledge, because we don't always know what to do with knowledge once we have it."

I remember the old proverb *a little knowledge is dangerous*, and knowledge without the ability to know what to do with it can also be dangerous.

I believe Walter had, all along through the years, known of his homosexual inclinations, but he had not known what to do with them. Attempting, while stewed to the gills, to seduce his best friend, who was equally a friend of his wife, attempting such a seduction in a public bar, was not very wise. From my point of view, since I never had the slightest physical desire for Walter, it might have been better if he had kept it simple and bought the male hustler. But who can keep it simple during a time of crisis, especially if you have to get drunk to expostulate the problem?

Walter's repressed homosexuality was too big for him to handle.

It was three days and three nights after the bar-room occurrence, shortly after sunset, that Walter went into the bathroom, stripped off while running a tub full of water, took a Gillette razor blade from its box, stepped into the nearly hot water, sat down, held his hand under the water and slit his wrist.

When Vera returned from the brief shopping and saw the bathroom door closed, she thought nothing of it, but while she began to put the groceries away, she felt an eerie wave of doom sweep over her. Something told her, she later said to me, that it was like the ghost of Walter had stepped out of the bathroom, floated over to her in the kitchen, and said to her, "Come and see me, Vera. I am dead."

She left the groceries where they were and rushed into the bathroom, and there in the bloody water, she saw her dead husband. She let out a scream, sharp and piercing, and then, "And then I knew, Phillip," she said to me, "I knew something I should have known for years, and probably deep down inside myself I did know but could not face as long as he was alive. Walter was gay."

Her scream apparently had cut into the screen she had tenaciously held up, the same screen he had held up, between them, a screen to hide that "stranger" inside himself. Now that he was dead, there was no longer any need for hiding.

"No, Vera, he was not gay. He was suffering from repressed homosexuality. The repressed homosexual is often a dangerous person. In Walter's case, he happened to be dangerous to himself."

"You don't think he ever did anything about it?" she asked. (This conversation was taking place after she had made the necessary emergency call to 911, and after they had taken his body to the morgue. She had telephoned me immediately after she had called 911, and I arrived not more than five minutes after them. We were talking in the dead silence that follows the removal of a corpse.)

"No. I am almost sure he did not."

"A few nights ago, when you brought him home, was it from a gay bar?"

"Yes, Vera."

"What happened?"

"Nothing actually happened."

"I've heard that sometimes things happen in the men's room of a gay bar."

"I doubt very much that anything like that happened with Walter. He might have watched something happening, but I don't think he would have joined in."

"Walter always admired you very much."

"Yes. You and Walter have been my closest friends for years, Vera. If there is anything I can possibly do to help you, you know I will."

"There's nothing you can do. You've already done it." She was speaking calmly, the calm after the storm, in a frozen voice. "You've helped my husband kill himself."

"You know that isn't true, Vera."

(I did not ask her, but the question ran through my mind: should I have taken Walter in my arms that night in Arty's Bar? Should I have taken him home with me and done the things he wanted to do? I couldn't. Would he have been alive now, if I had? Should I, I asked myself again, should I have bought the male hustler for him? I could not do these things for Walter. One man cannot live another man's life, even if trying to do so may save his life. Each man must save his own life, especially if it involves the sexual emotions.)

"I am seeing so many things now that I refused to see while he was alive. That stranger inside him was gay, or as you express it, he was a repressed homosexual."

"I think he was basically a bisexual, Vera, one who put aside, or rather put down, his feelings for others and gave them all to you. I have a feeling he was always faithful to you."

"Physically. But not emotionally."

"We can never possess another person entirely."

She seemed to ignore that remark. She spoke calmly, as calm as a slab of ice slowly floating down a stream: "He loved you, Phillip, in some ways more than he loved me. Not a day passed that he didn't talk about you, praising you as a writer, praising you and at the same time condemning you, as he repeatedly said you were too good for Terry Lane. I felt the same way about you, Phillip, so I did not let his feelings about you come through to me entirely. I blocked out what I did not want to see. I loved you as a friend. He loved you as a friend and he loved you as an unavailable lover. He envied you, he loved you; he hated you, he admired you. I can see it now, now that I'll never see him alive again, and I see how he was a mass of mixed emotions. What could he do with all those mixed up feelings? It would have taken a psychiatrist years to help him sort them out."

"He never wanted to know the whole truth about himself, Vera. He wanted to know the truth about the arts, but not about himself."

"He wanted to write, and he couldn't write. He almost idolized you because it seems to come so easy for you. He plodded and plodded, and nothing happened."

"It isn't always easy. Nothing is always easy. My lover is slowly dying from a stroke. My best friend has just killed himself."

She looked at me as if to quietly and politely remind me that my lover's wife had killed herself – two people in which my life was involved, were suicide victims.

The pit of my stomach seemed to cave in a little deeper. Could I have saved the life of Terry Lane's wife by giving up her husband? Could I have saved the life of Vera's husband by going to bed with him?

My flesh rankled and crawled.

By God, I had a right to love Terry!

And damn it to hell, I had a right to say "No" to Walter. I would have enjoyed sucking on the spine of a book as much as I would have enjoyed doing Walter. I think my senses would have gone blank if he had gone down on me.

"What in God's name did you mean, Vera, when you said I had helped Walter kill himself."

"Not directly. Indirectly. He wanted to be like you and he couldn't be like you. Now that he has gone, I can face that stranger inside of him. Walter vicariously lived on your sex life and your literary life. Walter was never truly himself. Tell me the truth, Phillip. I think I have a right to know. Did Walter try to seduce you that night in the barroom?"

I hesitated. If he were living I would have lied for him; now that he was dead, I saw no point in lying.

"Yes."

"And you turned him down."

"Yes."

"And so he killed himself."

There was a long silence, painful for me. But in this silence Vera seemed to be coming to some sort of terms with herself, her husband's death, and her life in the future.

"Stand beside me, Phillip. I know you will. Stand beside me until after the funeral. Then I am going back South. I never want to see or hear from you again, Phillip, once Walter is put away. Maybe I shouldn't hate you, but I do. Not intensely. It feels like a quiet, justifiable hatred that a respectable woman has a right to feel for someone who caused, even slightly, indirectly caused her husband to kill himself. I never again for the rest of my life want to discuss literature or even read a book. I think he loved that sort of thing more than he loved me. He loved you, in a way, he loved you more than he loved me."

Chapter 15

IT WAS SHAKESPEARE who said: *"When trouble comes it comes not as single spies, it comes in great battalions."*

Terry Lane's wife had killed herself. My beloved lover went wild. He became another man. He had a severe stroke, and he never again regained full consciousness. For two years he was an artificial man, not really a man, only a mass of flesh and bones that slightly resembled the love of my life.

Four years and ten days after his wife's suicide Terry Lane passed away in a nursing home in Sunnyside, Queens. That happened one week after Walter's suicide and Vera's quiet departure for Mississippi.

During the last two years of Terry Lane's existence, I would often go to him and sit at his bedside. I would read. I would listen to soft music. I would let my memory drift back to the times when we were in the ecstasy of each other's arms.

Occasionally I saw his sons as they were coming in and I was going out. I knew they did not visit him as often as I did. Why should they? They were too young to face such a lingering death in a man they had once known to be a vibrant father. On rare occasions I saw his sister. We spoke briefly or simply nodded. We did not pause for conversation. Something blocked us. Sometimes I thought I saw a question in her eyes. Why did you care so much about my brother? Sometimes I saw gratitude in her eyes.

The insurance agency covered eighty percent of the expenses for the first year. And that was all. I paid the remaining twenty percent for the first year and the full bill the second year. The sons had been financially forced to go to work immediately after graduation form high school. His sister lived with them and worked as a secretary in some sort of shipping firm. They barely got by. My books were selling well enough for me to cover Terry Lane's expenses during his last semi-living days. No. Those days and nights were not even semi-living. He was simply there. And so little of him was there.

It was one of those times of intimate memory that Terry opened his eyes and for the first time in two years recognized me. A slight, only very slight, smile curled the side of his lips that had not been paralyzed. The emeralds of his eyes almost shone again.

"You recognize me. Don't you, Terry? I see the recognition in your eyes."

He blinked his eyelids. The eyelids saying, Yes.

"I love you, Terry. I love you." I spoke in hardly more than a whisper, but the whisper came from my heart and soul.

I was holding his hand. I felt a slight pressure of response, as if the blood in his veins momentarily came to life again.

His emeralds gazed at me.

After a while, a mumbling sound came from his throat. His lips formed a single word: "*Love.*"

My lips trembled. Tears came into my eyes. I leaned over and kissed him.

He closed his eyes again.

He breathed heavily, as though the return to consciousness had been an effort. Then he drifted back into that comatose state.

Thirty-six hours later, while I was holding his hand, I felt his life drift away from him. Some part of it came into me, sank into my bloodstream and has flowed through me till this very day.

Chapter 16

The years went along, as years have a way of doing.
And we who are gay hunger with the years.

MY SEX LIFE had changed through time and tragedy. It had once, for those eleven blissful years, been a love life. Then when Terry went sexually mad, I was simply a part of the meat and cream he took to try to satisfy that wild hunger; only rarely did I go with anyone to quiet my own hunger. During the following two years that he was dying, I had anonymous sex. I discovered a glory-hole – the same one that he had used and told me about. It was between two cubicles in the men's room next to the cafeteria in the basement of a hospital. I went to the cafeteria once or twice a week, ostensibly to have dinner, but I knew in my blood it was to go into the men's room and anonymously still my sex drive. I would bare my ass, sit on the stool, and I usually did not have to wait long before a cock came through the hole, and I would quiet my oral desires. Then the same person or another person would put a faceless, nameless, unknown mouth to the hole, and I would stick my cock there and have my genital desires calmed. These acts gave me a form of excitement and semi-satisfaction. They never gave me thorough satisfaction. Too much was missing. It was a lonely kind of sex.

Three times during those two years, I took someone home with me, a different person each time. We embraced. We kissed. One of the guys expressed it very clearly when he said, "Thanks a lot. I wish you had been here. I enjoyed it. I always enjoy sex. But I would have enjoyed it a hell of a lot more if you had been with me. Man, you were far far away."

Three times of not being there, kisses that landed on the

flat surface of myself, three different guys – that was enough. The emptiness of myself hurt; the effort toward intimacy caused the emptiness to hurt even more. So the palm of my hand, or the glory hole calmed the sex drive down to some sort of unpainful loneliness. Terry's long time dying was painful enough. The pain of being with someone and still not being there was too much for me at that time.

Terry Lane was only in his early forties when all that beauty passed away – actually some of his beauty began passing away four years previously.

I was in my late thirties. My career had made progress. I was a known writer, and a known playwright, but not yet famous. I had had an artistic hit-commercial flop on Broadway and a reasonably successful off-Broadway hit. Young actors looked my way. Generally I looked the other way.

Time went along and so did my love for Terry Lane. After he physically passed away, the memory of our love grew more in my mind than the problems of the past four years.

A young actor moved in with me acting as if he loved me, but hoping most to obtain a role in my next play. The affair ended before the play was complete. I endured his bedroom auditions for two and a half months, they were pleasant, but his ego was up front on stage where there was no stage. He was attractive but his attractiveness could not compare with the remembered beauty of Terry Lane. Terry's ego had never been a problem. He gave me his beauty; he himself never wallowed in it.

I went back to the glory-hole and the reliability of the palm, but they were no longer enough for me. I don't suppose they ever had been enough. They had simply helped to tide me through those times of grief.

I started making pick ups. I tried, unintentionally, Terry's technique that he had used after his wife's death. Six months after Terry passed away and one month after the struggling actor was asked to move out, I went a little wild. Maybe it was more than a little. I went mad. I knew in my heart numbers were not what I wanted, but my mouth and my cock and my ass did not pay any attention to my heart.

I had wept quietly, and I had sobbed wrenchingly when

Terry passed away, but the memory had not passed away. I saw his two sons and his sister at the funeral, but the strange gaze in Terry, Jr's. emerald green eyes followed me long after the funeral. I soon forgot the younger son; I even forgot his name, and I soon forgot Terry's sister. I could not forget him.

Others came and went.

I almost loved one or two of them. It was not their fault I did not truly love them. Even when I was not thinking about it, my soul, my heart, my innards, remembered those eleven years of loving Terry Lane and Terry Lane loving me.

I almost loved others. But not quite.

After six months or so, the wildness of my sexual searches calmed down. I grew fairly content with brief non-love affairs, wherein neither of us were attempting to fall in love or live together or to establish any kind of lasting relationship. We would see each other for a few weeks, or a few months, for a few hours, enjoy it, and then go on to someone else, and someone else.

We had sex affairs instead of love affairs.

Yet my life was not without love. I have always loved my creative work, and I had the memory of Terry Lane.

You cannot live on memories. But they help.

I was in my early forties, forty-three to be exact, when a certain letter was forwarded to me from my publisher.

The letter read:

Dear Mr. Tucman,

I have read all your books and I have seen your two plays. I admire your work very much.

I am about to be engaged. At least, I think I am. I haven't asked my girl yet to marry me, but I know she will if I ask her. But I need an older man's advice.

I shall always miss my father. As you know, he passed away several years ago, and I shall always be grateful to you for standing by my father when he was so sick in that nursing home in Sunnyside.

I have a special reason for wanting to ask your advice. I'd rather do so in person. I can't write it and if you wrote your answer, it would not be the same.

Could I please see you and talk to you in person. Alone.

My telephone number is (there was a number written there).

Thank you, sir.

Sincerely yours,
Terry Lane, Jr.

Memories:

Oh, my God, the memories! How his son's letter brought back to me the memories of Terry.

For a few seconds my heart did not bother to beat. Then it thumped. Then it raced, raced memories through my heart and my mind, my soul and my bloodstream.

It had been years since Terry passed away, since the funeral. I had not seen or heard from his sons in five years. Terry, Jr. must be twenty-three, the same age as I was when my affair began with his father, who was, at the time, four years older than Terry, Jr. now.

How kind of him to choose me as a substitute father to give him advice.

I went to the telephone and called his number. This was on a Saturday that I received the letter, so I immediately made the call.

He answered, his voice sounding like his father's voice: "Hello".

In that one word I heard the tone of his father.

"My name is Phillip Tucman. Thank you for your letter. I just received it this morning."

"It's nice of you to call, and so soon. Sir?"

"Yes?"

"Is there a possibility I could see you? Alone? I don't want to talk over the telephone about what I need to know."

"Whenever you say."

"I have a date tonight, or I would ask for tonight. Or I can postpone the date. But maybe that would be too soon?"

"You don't need to postpone your date. What are you doing now? An hour from now."

"Nothing. You mean," he paused. "I could see you now,

this afternoon?"

"Of course." I gave him my address on the West Side of Manhattan in the Lincoln Center area.

"Oh, that's great. That's just great. Thanks a lot. It'll take me about an hour to get there. I'll get there sooner if I can."

My heart was pounding. My heart was racing. His voice sounded enough like Terry's to be Terry's. I stood by the telephone. Unconsciously, I was caressing the handle of the telephone. Terry Lane's voice. Terry Lane's son.

What should I be wearing when he arrives? House slippers or shoes. Casuals, I suppose. A sports shirt or a dress shirt? I chose a sports shirt. Shorts or briefs? Shorts. A pair of blue slacks. Terry had always liked me in blue. The light blue sports shirt. No undershirt. The dark blue slacks.

Did he drink. Most young people drank. Should I mix a batch of Martini's? Yes, I would do that. It would help the time to pass. I had been drinking too much recently. Being in one's forties seemed to increase a man's drinking. At least, that was an excuse. Good as any. But I would not get drunk or even high. I won't have even a drop, not a swallow, before he gets here. Terry Lane. Terry Lane, Jr. Terry.

His son's voice was the voice from the dead, the dead who never died, because memory would not let it die. Love would not let it die. I believed in that old saying, "True love never dies." It may go away. It may philander. It may be put in a casket, and the casket may be put in the ground, but the earth erupts with memories, and the memories are living thoughts in the heart and the mind and the blood and the soul of the lover.

Do the dead remember the ones they loved?

If you believe in the spirit, you know they do.

The memory of Terry Lane was caressing me; I had half a hard on when the door bell rang.

I opened the door.

I was astonished. He looked exactly like his father when I first met him, much more like him now than he did when his mother committed suicide, much more like him now than the few times I saw him in passing while his father was in the nursing home, much more like him now than he looked at his father's funeral. I was literally speechless. The pounding of my heart and the swirling of my memories took the place of speech.

He was smiling. His eyes were the eyes of jewels. His lips were the lips of – my God! What his father had done with lips like those lips!

"Hello," he said.

I simply stood there like a dumbfounded fool.

"I am Terry Lane, Jr."

Who else could he be...except Terry Lane himself?

"You said I could come to see you."

I was gazing into those emeralds and gazing into memory.

"May I come in?"

His hand had been reaching out to my hand to shake my hand. I had not been in sufficient contact with the reality of the moment to take his outstretched hand. Now his hand touched me on my forearm.

The touch awakened me, brought me to myself.

"Forgive me," I said. "You look so much like your father. So much. You struck me speechless."

I took his hand in my hand and held it, hardly shaking it, simply holding it, as though I were holding onto the flesh of memory, flesh that had been buried, memory that refused to be buried.

"Come in."

He could not come in. I was blocking the way. I did not have enough presence of mind to move out of the way.

He grinned. "May I?" And he took half a step closer to me.

I suppose I must have moved, slightly. Obviously I moved. I don't remember moving. I remember him being in the foyer; I remember saying: "You are your father all over again."

"Thank you. You knew my father very well, didn't you?"

Was there something implied in that question? An innuendo? The word *very*.

"Yes. We were the closest of friends for eleven, no, fifteen years. May I get you a drink?"

"No, thank you. I don't drink. Coffee or soda or something like that, if you don't mind."

"How about ginger ale?"

"Great."

"You don't mind if I have a Martini while you have your

more wholesome ginger ale?"

"Not at all."

His smile was incredible. It wavered his lips and sent out vibrations that could cause a Saint to tremble.

The Pope and I had never seen eye to eye, so it was not Sainthood that was trembling while I poured a Martini for myself and a ginger ale for Terry, Jr. My hands were trembling. My balls rolled by the years. When you are in your forties you are in your middle-age, so time tries to tell you, but my blood was telling me otherwise.

I spilled a few drops of the Martini on my wrist and licked it up.

He was standing in the middle of the living room, feeling a little awkward, I thought, and I thought he glanced at my crotch. Maybe I only dreamed it. Maybe I was really only mixing him up with his father.

"I gave him the glass of ginger ale. "Have a seat."

He sat on one end of the couch. I sat on the other.

There was a pause. I could hear him breathing. I could sense him working up his courage to say something.

"You... the way you said... eleven, no, fifteen years. What did you mean by that?" He asked the question as though he had to ask it but was afraid to ask it. He had to pull the question out of himself.

"Our friendship changed through the years. Time does that to life and to people. For eleven years we were..." and then I paused – how much should I tell him? – "we were the closest of friends. When your mother passed away, there was a change. We were still close, but he changed, he was hurt, and I felt his pain. Then two years later when he had his stroke, his lingering illness, the long drawn out time of dying, my pain was worse than his. As you know, he was in a comatose state most of that time."

"Yes. I never saw him come out of it. Did you?"

"Yes. Briefly. Very briefly. About a day and a half before he passed away, he came out of it for a few moments. It was as though the life instinct was making one last grasp."

"Did he recognize you?"

"Yes."

"Please. Tell me what he said."

I did not answer. I took a deep swallow of my Martini. How much could I tell him? How much did he want to know? How much did he need to know? What was his purpose in being here?

Instead of answering his question, I asked, "Is that why you wanted to see me? To ask what your father's last word was?"

"No. Not really. Not exactly."

"Why did you never ask before? Why didn't you ask at the funeral?"

"I don't know why I didn't ask. I think my brother and I and my Aunt believed he never came out of the coma."

"Only briefly. Very briefly."

"You don't have to tell me. Of course you don't. But it's only natural that I'd like to know what my father's last words were."

"There was only one word."

"Only one word?"

I took another deep swallow of my Martini. I made up my mind to tell him whatever he wanted to know. The years had passed. Although his presence was bringing them back again more vividly than I had experienced them in a long time. (So had the years really passed, or had they only receded somewhere inside my soul?)

"Yes," I said. "Only one word. The word was *love*."

There was a long pause.

I felt his eyes upon me. I did not look at him for a moment. I looked into the cocktail glass. But his gaze drew my eyes toward him. The emeralds were soft and glowing, a little sad, but somewhat relieved. I knew I could tell him anything he wanted to know. But he would have to ask. I could not make the first move of revelation. I could not simply throw the son into the father's past.

And so he asked, softly, "Were you and my father lovers?"

"Yes. We loved each other very very much."

"For all those years? Eleven years, I believe you implied, eleven years before my mother committed suicide?"

And I heard a tone of bitterness in his voice.

"And four years afterward."

"Did she know about those eleven years."

156

"Yes. She knew. Are you shocked?"

"No. I think I felt it all my life, felt it without knowing it. One time when I was about fourteen, Ronald, my brother, asked me if I thought our father was out with another woman those Sunday afternoons and evenings. I remember saying, 'It might not be a woman.' Ronnie said, 'Oh, just another guy.' He never suspected anything like..." he paused "...two men making love. But then for some reason the thought went out of my mind. Maybe not out of my mind, but somewhere into the back of my mind."

"He told her about his bisexuality before they were married. She accepted it. Or seemed to."

"Or seemed to, Mr. Tucman?"

"Call me Phillip. We never really know what is going on in another person's heart and mind."

"I have to be blunt. Tell me if you know... Did she kill herself because of that?"

I was afraid the conversation was getting to the reason for her suicide. Again I wondered how much should I tell him? Then an age-old belief, to which I try to adhere, came into mind: *honesty is the best policy*. Yet, it is also tremendously important the manner in which you express the policy.

"Your father and I loved each other very much."

"Yes."

I could not decipher from his tone or his expression whether he approved or disapproved. Certainly there was no violent objections. I gathered that he felt somewhere in between approval and disapproval, being the son of his father – the man who did the loving, and the son of his mother – the woman who did the killing of herself.

"Do you know what it is like for one man to love another?"

"Not exactly."

"Not exactly?"

"Well, I mean..."

"Speak freely. Speak freely with me so that I can speak freely with you."

"I've had a few guys go down on me. It was great. I trembled all over."

"That is pleasure. That is lust. That's good. But love goes far far beyond the flesh. When you are in love the heart is capable of having a spiritual orgasm. Your father and I shared many physical orgasms together. We shared even more spiritual orgasms. While we were together and even while he was in Brooklyn and I was in Manhattan. We loved each other very very much."

"I don't suppose," he sipped his ginger ale, gazed at the bubbles, and said, "I don't suppose a person can blame another person for loving, or how he loves."

"Thank you, Terry. Your father would appreciate that feeling."

"If my mother knew from the very beginning, if she knew, then why did she kill herself? Do you know? Did my father know?"

"He believed it was because of him. He tortured himself with guilt for two years after her death. Then the stroke incapacitated him, but took away the torture."

"But if she knew, all those years, why did she turn against herself?"

"She thought he had turned against her. But he hadn't. His desire for her lessened, even went away. It often does that to many married couples, living together day after day, night after night, year after year. When he no longer desired her, she thought he no longer loved her. But he never stopped loving her. She was the mother of his two sons whom he loved very much."

"You mean she misinterpreted his feelings?"

"Suicide is often a misinterpretation of life."

"But he never stopped loving her?"

"Never. Not even after her death. And I have never stopped loving your father. Not even after his death. All these years. Death changes love, but it does not end love. I have tried to love others, and perhaps to some small degree, I have, but your father was the greatest love of my life."

Then from out of the blue, out of the depths, from out of a dream, he said:

"Do with me what you did with my father. Just once. I want to see what it is like. I want to feel the reason my father loved you so much. Tell me the things he did with you, and let me do all those things. I've never gone all the way with anyone. I want to experience it before I definitely decide to

158

ask my girl to marry me. Am I foolish or am I wise?"

"You are beautiful."

I don't think I cared whether he was foolish or wise.

Terry was with me again. The seed of Terry was Terry, Jr.

"Will you?"

"Of course I will."

"I want to know how much of my father is in me. I don't know if I have to know, but I want to know. I need to know."

"You did not learn those things from the others who went down on you?"

"No. Each time it happened I thought about you. I thought about asking you years ago. But I never worked up the courage. Who can teach me more about my father's intimate feelings, who but my father's lover?"

I had sat my Martini on the cocktail table; he had sat his ginger ale beside my empty cocktail glass. The space between us disappeared and he was in my arms. I did not have to imagine Terry was with me again. Terry, Jr. was the extension of Terry. I drew the son's tongue into my mouth and it was the same as his father's tongue. Momentarily the years between us disappeared as surely as the space on the couch had disappeared. Our tongues rolled. I inserted my tongue into his mouth, and I once again inserted my soul into paradise. My hand went to his crotch, and the hardness of his organ softened the time between the time with his son and the last times with the father – before the mother had killed herself and killed something inside my lover who could not die because he lived in my memory and he lived in the genes, the cells, the blood and the beauty of the son now in my arms, the son who was feeling my crotch, the son who was fumbling so beautifully with my zipper. The living extension of Terry was removing the extension of my stalk of love, taking it out of my fly, and quickly, as if a ghost had pushed him, his head fell into my lap, and he went down on me to the very root of my joint.

Is it possible for a son to inherit his father's technique?

That tongue of years ago swept down through the years and swept my flesh again.

He stopped. He must have sensed I was about to come. He stopped and said, "Please take me to bed."

I could not speak. I simply took that magnificent tongue into my mouth and sucked upon it, and still sucking, we slowly stood. Then the separation of our mouths was almost painful. I could see a startled expression in his eyes, and I heard him say, "I never expected it to be so great."

I could feel tears of joy in my eyes. Words were stuck in my throat and in my heart. My joint was standing up and out of my fly. I did not put it away. We went into the bedroom.

"Let me undress you." I could speak again.

As I removed each article of clothing, I kissed his bare flesh, and I remembered the first time I had done this with his father. The son's flesh was the flesh of the father, and so I kissed the reality of time and I kissed the memory of time.

His young chest was bare, and I sucked upon his tits, and the trembling of his body silently echoed the trembling of his father's body. Even the slight hair upon his chest seemed to be spaced the same as his father's.

I sank to my knees in front of him and removed his shoes and socks while his hands played in the hairs of my head, and he whispered the name of God: "Oh God, my God, my God, my God my God" as if he were praying to God in Heaven and giving thanks for this time of paradise upon the earth of man.

I unbuckled his belt and pulled down his zipper, and his trousers fell, and my face pressed against the magnificent bulge in his briefs. I pulled his briefs down, and my hands went to his buttocks and my mouth went down upon an uplifted dream in the flesh, and I was filled again with paradise unlike any earthly pleasure I had known since before the death of this young man's mother. The seed of him came from his father's cock, a cock I had known hundreds of times, and that seed entered the darkness of his mother, where my lover had planted it, and the seed grew and grew until it became a man, and now the man brought the grown seed to me, and I sucked upon this staff of heaven, and perhaps his father up in Heaven looked down upon us and smiled as we relished paradise.

"Don't make me come yet," he was gasping words of extreme delight, as he pulled back his buttocks and removed his cock from my mouth.

"Turn around and bend over," I said.

Without hesitation he did as I asked, and my face went between his buttocks even as my face had buried itself between the buttocks of his buried father, and my tongue went to his asshole, and I sucked away the time between the father and the son, and they were neither the one nor the other, for I sucked time clean of the pain that it plunges into our lives, and I wiped away the years, and there were no years – there was simply these moments of bliss.

The son became the father, and the father became the son, and I ascended unto heaven in a fiery chariot of dreams, and heaven turned and gave me its staff again and said unto me, "I can't wait, take me, take me," and I took the staff of heaven unto me, to the very depths of me, and heaven poured its liquid fires into me, and I was blessed with the son of my love for the spirit of the father had never left me.

His hands almost crushed my head against his crotch, and then in the silence that comes after the emptying of fluid, he spoke as though we were answering a question he had harbored in his young soul for years: "My father had a right to love you."

I wept upon his belly.

He was still standing; I was kneeling on the floor. We had not had the time to go to bed. We were simply there beside the bed.

He felt my tears upon his flesh. He sank to his knees there beside me and kissing my tears, he drank my tears. "Why are you weeping?" he asked.

I had to kiss his sweet mouth again before I answered his question. So as I kissed it again and again, and I saw a tear from my eyes roll into his mouth.

"You are your father all over again. I was never aware, I was never conscious of feeling any guilt about your father loving me and the tragedy that happened. But hearing you say in the nakedness of yourself that your father had a right to love me, hearing those beautiful words, washes clear any stains upon the past. I loved him so very much."

His fingers examined my face and slowly caressed my lips. His eyes, the jewels, the emeralds, gazed into my eyes, and after a while he said, "We haven't even gone to bed yet. Will you take me to bed with you?"

"Yes," I whispered, and we laughed soft laughter as we lifted ourselves upon the bed where I lay upon my back and he lay half upon me and half upon the bed. And he rested his head upon my shoulder and gazed down upon my loins as my mind intermingled the son and the father. He was caressing the hairs around my cock.

After a few moments, I asked, "What are you thinking?"

"About my father's mouth on your cock. Did he do it very many times?"

"Many times."

"How many times?"

"Thousands of times. At least five thousand times."

"Five thousand times. Five thousand times he drank from you."

"Yes."

"He loved you."

"He loved me."

"I understand my father." And in saying these words his tongue went across and down my chest to my waist and to my belly and he took the head of desire into his mouth and let his tongue go around it, and then he took it out and gazing upon it, he asked, "Did my father do it this way?"

"Yes. Your father did it many ways."

"It's big."

"Yes. So is yours. Just like your father's."

"Did he like taking all of it?"

"Yes."

And with that the son of my beloved went all the way down upon it and held the root with tender passion between his teeth as if he would eat it and swallow it and make it entirely his own, but he let up on it and came up to the head of it and down again, and I knew he was in a spiral of ecstasy, and it was this my flesh giving him the ecstasy, and my soul went up into the heavens, and my spirit kissed the spirit of the father in paradise while the son gave heaven to my earthly flesh.

We were a gay and holy trinity.

We were sacred unto ourselves and sacred unto the memory.

162

We went beyond tragedy and I came in his mouth, the living mouth of my deceased lover's son. He swallowed the cream of my body, the cream of my life.

He took my cock out of his mouth and gazed at it. He squeezed it and another large drop emerged upon the head of it.

"May I have that?" he asked.

"Yes."

And so he took it.

And then he rested his head upon my lower belly, even as his father had rested his head on the same spot, and I felt his breath breathing into my pubic hairs, even as I had felt his father's breath breathing into the hairs around my staff of life.

Then, with the regeneration of youthful energy, he said, "Turn over for me."

So it was as I was turning over, before I was even flat upon my belly, his tongue was seeping into my asshole, and he rimmed me even as his father had rimmed me and as I had rimmed the father years ago and as I had rimmed the father's son moments ago.

Asses of heaven. Asses of paradise.

Earthly asses.

We were in the magnificence of ourselves. We gave, we received, we shared the heights and the depths of ecstasy. The son of my beloved probed between my buttocks with a hunger that I had not known since the tongue of his father.

"Did my father like this?"

"Your father loved it."

The intensity of his sucking increased as I spoke.

He ravished my ass. He savored my hole. He was as a man who had thought of the food of his father for years, and the thought became a dream, and the food and the dream and the mouth of the father and the mouth of the son became as one in the union of oral-anal passion.

"My father's mouth was here?"

"Yes."

"My father's tongue was here?"

"Yes."

Hearing of his father's hunger, enhanced his hunger.

"Did my father fuck you in your asshole?"

"Your father fucked me many times in my asshole."

"Tell me to do the way my father did. Tell me anything and everything."

"Crawl on top of me, and while I split the cheeks of my buttocks slide your cock inside me. Fuck me to your heart's content."

"Oh, my God! My father in heaven, I'm going to fuck your lover in his ass."

He whispered those words as his tongue left my ass and travelled up my spine, and he crawled on top of me, and I slightly lifted my hips as he inserted the divine meat of himself deep inside me. I clenched my buttocks several times around the rod of my lover's son.

"You did that to my father while he did this to you?"

He plunged.

"Yes, my son. Yes."

Why did I call him "my son"? He was not my son, he was Terry Lane's son. But if it had been possible he would have been my son.

Even his rhythm was the rhythm of his father. And when he came into me the sound of his gasping was the sound of one who had departed from this earth in a physical way but was still with me deep in my soul even as his son was deep in my ass.

After a few moments, while he was still inside me, the son spoke into my ear: "My father loved you because he had to love you. I understand my father now so much more than I did during his lifetime. I suspected, but I don't like suspicions. I needed to know, I had to know. I'm glad I know. I know where he was those Sunday afternoons and evenings. I'm glad it was not another woman."

"Your father never had another woman after he married your mother."

"He had you."

"He had me."

"Is it natural to love another man like this?"

"Love is always natural."

"Now, at this moment, I love you. But how will I feel tonight? I have a date with my girl tonight. How will I feel tomorrow?"

164

"I cannot say. Tonight and tomorrow will answer those questions for you."

"However I feel, however I am going to feel, I know how my father felt, and that is something I have wanted to know for as long as I can remember. Did my father sometimes do this? – linger inside you and talk with you."

"Your father and I had many conversations while his cock lingered in my ass. And the spirit of your father lingers in my heart and soul, and that part of him, some part of him, shall always be inside me. We loved each other very much. The spirit of his love will never die."

"That's beautiful."

He was making slight movements. His penis had grown almost, but not quite, limp; now it was growing hard again.

"May I do it again?" he whispered.

"You are your father all over again. Do it again."

... And so later he said, when he was dressed and he was at the door, that is when he said, "I'll call you."

Inside me had asked: "How will I feel tonight? How will I feel tomorrow?"

I did not see or hear from him for three weeks. Then one evening when I picked up the telephone I heard his voice: "This is Terry. Terry Lane, Jr."

"I've been wondering about you. How are you?"

"I've been wondering about myself and thinking about you."

"I'm glad you called."

Then bluntly: "I married my girl last week. We were away on a week's honeymoon. We just got back."

"Oh." That's all I could say. A sort of dry *Oh*.

"I thought it was only decent that I should call and tell you."

I was silent. Apprehensive. Expectant.

"I liked it too much. Being with you, I mean. I loved it too much. Try to understand me. Let me tell you. To relieve my conscious. To help me know who I am. With you, it was beyond pleasure. I had sex with my girl that night. That was sexual pleasure. I am an ordinary guy. Being with you, doing what you and my father did, that was extraordinary. I think it would drive me out of my mind. I mean, actually, honestly, I believe I would go crazy doing it that way if I did it very much, very often. Maybe I should not be calling you now. Maybe I should not be even telling you anything. My wife is in the tub. Taking a bubble bath. Like my mother. My mother took bubble baths. I don't blame my father. I don't blame my father for anything. I don't blame you. But I think if my wife ever killed herself, I would blame myself. So maybe I shouldn't have married. But I had to. I mean I thought I had to. With you, with you, Phillip, no, let me call you Mr. Tucman, it will help me put a space between us. With you I thought I was giving my soul away when I came inside you, and what would a man do without his soul? I shot the spirit of myself inside you, not just my cum, but my spirit, and I drank your spirit. If we were lovers, if I became entirely like my father, I would not be me. I don't think I know who I would be. Oh, my God, Phil – no, I mean, Mr. Tucman – it's okay with my wife. It's okay. It's pleasant. I just don't think I can take heaven. Let me say it once, than I pray to God I'll forget you: I love you. Good-bye. Forgive me. I loved it too much. I'll never do it again. Never."

And he hung up.

I never heard from him again. Not directly.

Chapter 17

THAT WAS YEARS AGO

How many years ago? Approximately twenty.

Where does the time go. It goes with the cum.

How many have there been since Terry, Jr.? There have been hundreds: quickies, brief encounters, short affairs. The longest lasted a year. The shortest lasted three minutes.

I don't think I really tried to form another lasting relationship. The one that lasted a year was primarily due to the efforts of the other guy involved. He wanted an involvement. He needed to be wanted by the same man, not by many men. Still it faded away when he met someone who wanted him more than I did. We parted friends. Others accused me of being self-centered. Some said I was lost in a fog. And there were others who perceived the truth: "You seem to be away somewhere in a dream."

Even when I was not aware of it my blood was dreaming of Terry Lane and Terry, Jr.

Terry Lane was the great love of my life. That one afternoon with his son became a part of it, an extended, regenerated, bloodline part of it.

So the years go along. They go with a heart full of memories. My passions have not disappeared. They have faded down but not away. As I awake in the mornings, before I am fully awake, half in a dreamstate, my mind goes back to Terry or Terry, Jr. The beauty I have known gives intimate meaning to my life.

I am in my early sixties. I can hardly believe it. We change so much through the years. Fortunately, I have not grown fat, although there is something of a bulge in my belly, but I can sometimes hide that by pulling in my belt another notch and holding up my shoulders, especially if I am wearing a sweater or a jacket, and if I am flat on my back in the nude, it doesn't show.

Listen to me, youngsters. Do not toss my memories aside yet. If you live, you'll reach my age too. It's not so bad. It's called maturity.

There is only a touch of grey in my hair, but more lines of experience in my face than I care to mention. (They are rudely known as wrinkles, and all the face creams and lotions in the world do not put a stop to them. However, sweethearts, I have discovered a lotion that makes my skin feel soft for hours after using it. Write to me, and I'll tell you what it is.) I look into my mirror and I see more of my yesterdays than I see today.

And my story of Terry Lane and Terry Lane, Jr. has not yet ended. It is not only that my memory of them has never come to an end, something else has been added. Time goes on extending itself.

Numbers of times through the years I have received letters – sent to my publishers and forwarded to me – from young writers or would-be-writers asking me to read their work. Generally time does not permit. However, a few days ago there came to me in the mail a letter that held my attention, stirred my soul, revitalized my memories, caused my heart to pound with the beats of youth, and gave warmth to my blood.

Dear Mr. Tucman,

My father has a collection of all your books, your plays and your two volumes of poetry. He reads them over and over again. He tells me you are his favorite author, and I think you are becoming my favorite author too. I have read all your books and I expect to reread them.

I am a writer too. At least, I think I am a writer. No, I know I am a writer. I haven't been published yet, but I know I will be some day.

I am twenty, and I have just completed my first short novel, or maybe it's a long story. I love it. My mother and father think it is great. My father suggested that I contact you and that maybe you could be of some help to me, some way. He said he met you before I was born and spent an afternoon with you just two weeks before I was conceived. Mother says I was conceived on their wedding night. Mother says I look just like my father. So maybe you will remember my father if you consent to see me and read my work. My father says you knew my Grandfather very well and was a close friend of his for years and years. I never knew my Grandfather. He passed away before I was born. But my father says I look just like my Grandfather.

I would like to meet you and talk with you. I believe I could learn a lot about writing by just talking with you, but not only about writing, about life too. There are so many things I wonder about. My father is a very understanding person. I love him very much. But there are some things I'd rather not talk to him about. Something inside me tells me I could, if you will agree, talk to you about anything and everything. You are such an experienced author, please let me meet you.

Sincerely yours,
   (his name was signed here)
   Terry Lane, III

Oh, my God!
The grandson of my dreams, the grandson of my most beautiful lover, the grandson of my heart.
Dear God, is my heart strong enough to take it? Whether I can take it or not, I'll damn well try it. If I die from cardiac arrest at the sight of a third generation of magnificent beauty, then what better way to go. Oh, my God, my God, give me strength! Give this man of years, sixty-three, the strength to see it through. Don't let me dribble. Don't let me pass out. Let me, let me... whatever, God, just let me.

He had not given me a telephone number, perhaps an oversight. The letter came from Brooklyn. I could have looked in the telephone directory and found the number, but I did not want to talk with his mother – mothers or wives of my lovers or potential lovers usually turn me off. I avoid them to the best of my ability. And suppose his father answered? I would have liked that too much. And his father wanted to forget me. Yet he had made a collection of my books. He had suggested to his son that he contact me. But I reminded myself that if his father, now in his early or mid forties, wanted to contact me, he could have done so at any time. I maintained a policy of never stirring up a married man unless he stirred himself up first.

Did Terry Lane, Jr. have more than literary reasons for suggesting to his son that he contact me? Did he want his son to examine himself or be examined in that area of gay life?

I wrote Terry Lane, III a brief note, letting him know I would be glad to meet with him and talk with him. I gave him my telephone number.

Three days later he called me.

It might have been his Grandfather, risen from the dead, calling me and wanting to see me, their voices were so much alike. His Grandfather would be sixty-eight or sixty-nine, if he had lived. The young man calling me was barely twenty. I heard an echo of past dreams in his voice. And there was a tone of excitement. I told myself I must not fool myself. Was the excitement in his voice because he was about to meet with a somewhat famous author? I know how I would have felt if I had had the opportunity to meet an author when I was his age, an author who had actually been published. I told him he could come over this evening if he wished, and I gave him instructions as to how to reach my place.

I had grown tired of the high-rise in Lincoln Center in Manhattan, and I had bought a private home in Sunnyside, Queens with a front porch and actually a front yard where I grow roses as red as Terry Lane's moist lips and as red as a certain other part of Terry Lane – the man who gave me these memories – the man whose son gave me a few intimate hours of bliss – the man whose grandson was on his way to see me.

At six-thirty I went on my front porch and waited with my dog Duchess, waited for the young man who was not due until seven-thirty. This was the month of June, twilight would be setting in at the time of his arrival. Actually I felt as if I were in my twilight years, not old but apprehensively older. I had heard of younger men who preferred older men and had been with a few in quick episodes. However, most of us are taking care more than we are taking to the bed.

170

Nevertheless, I keep a supply of rubbers on hand. I call them dream rubbers. And everyday I pray to God that the doctors, research people, scientists, whoever, someone, may find a prevention and cure for this plague that has come down upon this world of passion. I have known the years of free-flowing passion, and the years have served me well. So it is more for the young people that my heart aches and my prayers go out to them. Still we may love, even though we must flow with care.

The Duchess, my German Shepherd, sits up and perks up her ears. She sees a stranger coming down the street. I can see the stranger has blond hair. And as he comes nearer to me, he no longer appears as a stranger. He is the reproduction of his father and his grandfather. Only there is something about him that is slightly different. Just as the senses of a dog can frequently sense things that we humans can't, we gay people can frequently sense something in others that may be known only to ourselves. There is something about the walk of Terry Lane the Third that tells me he is probably not a bisexual, and he is certainly not a heterosexual – I have a feeling that he is full-blown gay.

Oh, my God! will he want me? Not just my literary opinions, but my intimate experience.

He is wearing such tight blue jeans I can see he is hung as well as his father and his grandfather.

My God, My God! I pray for the younger generation in more ways than one.

He is carrying a manuscript in his left hand.

He stops at the gate. He looks at me here on my porch, and he smiles. His lips, his mouth. His father, his grandfather.

The Duchess barks.

"Hush, Duchess. Hush."

He opens the gate and he walks toward me.

I am sitting with my legs spread apart.

My eyes glance at his crotch.

His eyes, his emerald green eyes, glance where I want his lips to be.

Memories are swirling in my mind; memories are beating in my heart.

And thank God, I am still young enough to gather up new memories.

Stephan Gray
BORN OF MAN

In Johannesburg, South Africa, in October 1987, amidst the hysterical attentions of local people and the media, an epoch-making breakthrough in medical science took place; the birth of a baby girl to a man! This sensational episode is brilliantly brought to life in Stephan Gray's latest novel. The drama unfolds in a series of comic escapades, in which 'mother' Kevin becomes tangled in a triangle of romantic intrigue.
The story is narrated by a nameless insider, whose humour and high camp can not disguise the horrors of apartheid. This extraordinary tale, rich in eloquence and observation, comes from the acclaimed author of last year's *Time of Our Darkness*. But *Born of Man* represents a major advance, breaking away from conventional notions of how a 'comic' novel should read.

'Stephan Gray braids real, idiosyncratic lives of South Africans rather than symbols, giving us truths of a very high order, since they are so alive, so personal' - Kurt Vonnegut

'Gray's strength is that he does not deal in dark metaphors, but accepts South African society as it is and, without special pleading, depicts the way in which its inhabitants cope with that society' - Peter Parker, *London Magazine*

ISBN 0-85449-107-4   208pp   Price: £4.95

Mike Seabrook
UNNATURAL RELATIONS

For Jamie Potten, burdened at fifteen with a bullying father and an uncaring mother, his encounter with 19-year-old Chris brings solace and joy. Chris' love for Jamie, however, leads to his prosecution of 'buggery with a minor,' carrying still today a potential sentence of life imprisonment.

In this gripping yet tender story of two young people facing together a brutal assault on their human rights, Mike Seabrook highlights and challenges the iniquitous position of gay teenagers under English law. This positive novel is both an important contriubtion to gay rights, and should prove essential reading for young gays, uncertain of their position in society.

An author of many disciplines, Mike Seabrook has written everything from cricket essays to a controversial insider's account of the British police force. *Unnatural Relations* should now firmly establish his talent as a novelist.

ISBN 0-85449-116-3   288 pages   Price: £5.95

Kenneth Martin
BILLY'S BROTHER

When Billy dies in mysterious circumstances, his brother comes to San Francisco to try and uncover the truth of his death, and is immediately drawn into the network of AIDS sufferers and support groups that Billy had been part of. Among them, he is sure the clue to Billy's death will be found - but he is unprepared for the other revelations that his investigation unveils.

Kenneth Martin is the author of *Aubade*, a remarkable first novel of teenage innocence first published in 1957 and written when Martin was just sixteen - this has recently been revived in our Gay Modern Classics series. *Billy's Brother* represents Martin's first new novel in almost thirty years, and could not be further removed from the experiences depicted in *Aubade*. It is a sharply observed mystery thriller, dealing with the changes AIDS has brought to everyone's lives, and raising important questions about the ways in which we all respond to its existence.

ISBN 0-85499-109-0   *208 pp*   *Price: £4.95*

GMP books can be ordered from any bookshop in the UK, and from specialised bookshops overseas. If you prefer to order by mail, please send full retail price plus £1.50 for postage and packing to; GMP Publishers Ltd (GB), PO Box 247, London N17 9QR. (For Access/Eurocard/Mastercard/American Express/Visa give number and signature.) Comprehensive mail-order catalogue also available.

In North America order from Alyson Publications Inc, 40 Plympton St, Boston MA 02118, USA

Name and Address in block letters please:

NAME _____

ADDRESS _____

_____

_____

_____